DEATH BY DI

CAPE COD COZY M

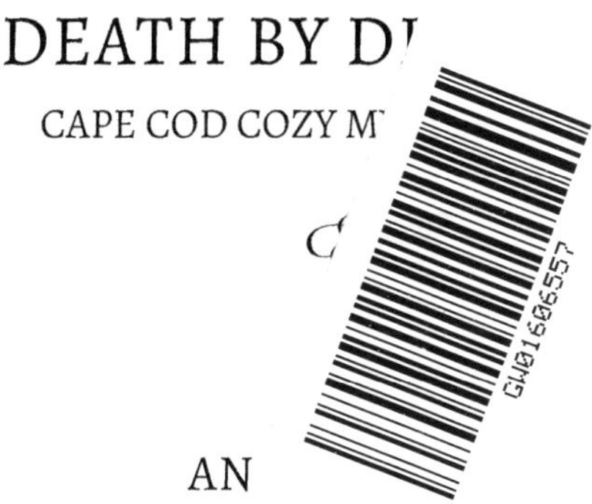

C

AN

JOHN PAUL PUBLISHING

Death by Driftwood/Angela K. Ryan. -- 1st ed.

ISBN: 979-8-9913260-9-4

CHAPTER 1

Cassie peered through the kitchen window above the sink of her freshly bought Cape Cod beach house and scanned Starboard Lane for the umpteenth time.

"You are going to wear a path from the living room to the kitchen if you don't stop pacing," Sydney said. "Your friend probably just hit some of that infamous Cape Cod summer traffic."

"I doubt that. It's Monday and most tourists arrive on Saturday. Besides, it's not even Memorial Day weekend yet. There's shouldn't be any traffic coming onto the Cape right now." Cassie sighed. "I hope she gets here before you leave for your meeting. You're going to love her. She was my first friend..."

Sydney plopped back down in the armchair and finished Cassie's sentence. "I know. Anna McBride was your first friend, besides Mary Beth, who you met after losing your memory in the car accident two months ago. I can't wait to meet her, but you're making me anxious with all your pacing."

Cassie ignored Sydney's complaint. "She was kind to me at

a time when so many people treated me with suspicion. Including Jake. In fact, she was the inspiration for all my amateur sleuthing. I was attending a party in her ice cream shop in Seagull Cove when a teacher at the local high school was murdered down the street. I helped her solve the case back in February. When I called her a few weeks ago and told her that my memory returned, she insisted on visiting me in person to celebrate."

As soon as Cassie returned to the living room and sat on the couch, she heard a car engine in the driveway. Her half Shih Tzu and half Maltese puppy Artie trotted to the front door from his favorite sunny spot by the sliding glass door in the living room, wagging his tail.

The car door thumped as it closed. Cassie threw open the front door to find Anna bounding up the walkway. The two women embraced.

"Cassie!" Anna cried, tying her long brown hair into a ponytail as she stepped back to look at her friend. "You look fantastic."

The women embraced again, then Cassie took Anna inside and introduced her to Sydney, who was eagerly awaiting the introduction. Anna gave Sydney a warm hug, which Sydney returned.

"Cassie told me what great friends the two of you have become in such a short time," Anna said. "See, Cassie? I knew things would work out for the best."

"I couldn't see it when I was in Seagull Cove, but if that horrible accident had to happen anywhere, I'm so glad it was here."

"I can't believe you ended up settling in Sand Dune Shores, after all," Anna said. "If that's not fate, I don't know what is."

"We'll get you checked in at the *Sand Dune Inn* in a little while, but first, come and visit with Sydney for a few minutes. She just purchased the cutest little Cape-style house a few streets over, and she needs to scoot back home to meet the woman who is measuring the windows for curtains."

"I thought I'd splurge on new window treatments and a couple of light fixtures to make it my own. The previous owner recently did a major renovation, but I wanted to personalize it beyond just furniture and pictures."

"That sounds exciting," Anna said.

They sat in the living room, which was only about thirty yards from the Atlantic Ocean during high tide. Anna scratched the top of Artie's head. "I heard all about you, little fellow. I thought you might like this." She reached into her purse and tossed the pup a chew toy.

"You've made a friend for life," Cassie said, laughing.

Anna leaned toward Sydney. "It's weird calling her Cassie, isn't it? We both met her as Heather."

"It did take some getting used to. I still slip and call her Heather sometimes."

It was mid-May but there was still a chilly breeze coming off the Nantucket Sound, so Cassie made some hot chocolate for her company. Sydney had tons of questions about Anna's ice cream shop back in Seagull Cove, a quaint seaside town on the North Shore of Boston. Anna had closed her counseling practice in the city and opened her shop a few years after her sister passed away in a tragic boating accident.

Sydney told Anna about her career as a children's book author and how she had been renting the beach house that Cassie now owned. "Cassie basically took over my life," Sydney said with a playful smile. "Artie used to be my dog, but

I gave him to Heather—I mean, Cassie—she was Heather at the time. The timing wasn't right for me to adopt a dog. Once her memory returned, and she realized she could afford it, she bought this beach house, which I had been renting while I looked for a house."

"You two certainly have packed a lot of adventure into two months," Anna said.

"That doesn't even count the four murders that she solved," Sydney said.

In a way, it seemed like a lifetime ago that Cassie came to Sand Dune Shores. So much had happened in the past two months. Her memory returned nearly a month ago, but since then, she went back to Colorado for a couple of weeks to ship her belongings and say goodbye to some friends. She also made a detour to Iowa to investigate the case that brought her to Cape Cod.

"I want to hear all about your trip home and your side trip to Des Moines," Anna said.

Sydney stood and grabbed her purse. "That's my cue to go. I've heard all about it, and I don't want to be late for my meeting. But let's definitely spend some time together while you're here. I'd love to have you over for dinner at my new house. I just unpacked the last box last night."

"Thank you," Anna said. "I'll look forward to it."

"Your new home is amazing," Anna said after Sydney left. "You must be a very successful artist to be able to afford this house."

"I've been blessed. Let's go for a walk before it gets too cold, and I'll catch you up on everything," Cassie said. "Then I'll give you the grand tour and get you checked in at the inn.

Are you sure you don't want to stay with me? I have plenty of room."

"I appreciate the offer, but the inn is right across the street. I'm only staying a few nights, so I thought I'd treat myself."

"If you change your mind, there's plenty of space here. It's a tiny beach house, but there are three bedrooms."

Anna looked through the sliding glass door onto the beach just beyond. "Will do. For now, I really want to explore that beach."

Cassie put on a black fleece sweatshirt, then picked up Artie's leash. He immediately abandoned his chew toy and trotted over to Cassie. "Let's go, buddy," she said, fastening his leash.

When they stepped onto the deck, Anna stopped and admired the view. "You are going to love sitting here in the summer," she said, gazing at the ocean.

"I know. I can't wait. We've had a few warm days, but the summer months are going to be incredible here." Memorial Day was the following weekend, which was when Cassie was told the tourists would start arriving.

The women turned past the massive sand dune on the left and followed the shoreline.

"Is that a sandbar?" Anna asked, pointing to a shallow area a short distance from the shore.

Cassie nodded. "I hear it's a fun spot to hang out during those August heat waves."

They continued walking for ten minutes until they arrived at a small inlet and couldn't go any further without getting wet. On their way back, a man with greying dark hair wearing blue jeans and a navy polo sweatshirt waved at them from the top of the dune. They walked toward him, but stopped in front of a sign that read, 'Stay off the Dunes.'

The man made his way toward them, toting an armful of weathered driftwood.

"That's beautiful wood," Anna said.

He looked over his shoulder, then hopped off the dune.

"Anna, meet Darren Germain. He makes the most beautiful driftwood art you've ever seen. Darren, this is my good friend, Anna McBride."

Darren smiled proudly at the mention of his art. "I have a little studio and showroom on the edge of town. If you'd ever like to take a look at some of my pieces, Cassie knows where to find me."

"I might take you up on that. I own a little cottage in Seagull Cove, and I'm looking for something to go on my mantle."

"Darren's work is exquisite. I'm going to buy a piece for my art studio once I finish setting it up."

"I'll tell you what. Since you're a friend of Cassie, I'll give you my friends-and-family discount—ten percent off your first purchase."

Anna smiled. "Thank you. That's very generous."

He raised his eyebrows. "I'd better go before you-know-who finds me. Besides, I have a houseguest who should be arriving about now." He rolled his eyes slightly. "Once you become successful, everyone wants a piece of you." He left via the public entrance, about twenty yards beyond Cassie's house.

"What did he mean by you-know-who?" Anna asked after he left.

"He was talking about Maya Deveau. She's a local environmentalist who calls the police whenever she sees him climbing on the dunes."

"She's not wrong," Anna said. "If everyone did that, they would erode."

"I agree, but I didn't want to rock the boat, since I just moved here. Maya seems like she has the situation under control. She snapped a picture of him on the dune last month, and he was slapped with a hefty fine. From what Sydney told me, he doesn't do it nearly as often now. He must need the wood to create inventory for the tourist season."

Cassie and Anna made their way back to the beach house. Cassie unfastened Artie's leash once they cleared the dune. The puppy raced up the steps to the deck and sat by the slider wagging his tail.

When they stepped inside, Cassie gave Anna a tour of her new home, though Anna had already seen most of it while they were talking with Sydney. The small kitchen opened into an area just big enough for a four-person table, and the living room had just enough room for a comfy couch and a reclining chair. There were three small bedrooms and a bathroom off the main living area. Cassie had settled into the largest bedroom, which faced the beach.

"The other unit has the same layout, just mirrored," Cassie explained. "I'm turning it into an art studio. Come on, I'll show you."

They exited through the front door, which faced the inn. The front yard of the weathered grey duplex, which contained sand instead of grass, was enclosed by a white picket fence. There was a sandy path between the two units that lead to the beach. They were connected by a roof, so you had to go outside to access the second unit.

"Someday I might combine the two units into one large living space. But before I spend any more money, I want to live in it for a while. The other advantage to keeping the units separate is that places on the beach command a hefty sum for short-term summer rentals. If I ever needed the extra cash, I could rent it out and it wouldn't impact my own living space."

"It's smart not to rush into any changes," Anna said. "I know it's well into the future, but if you plan to make this your forever home, it could be a nice source of income after you retire."

Cassie hadn't had time to decorate her art studio yet, except for a few of her paintings that she hung on the walls. There were still boxes of art supplies and wrapped paintings to sort through. She had placed a blank canvas on an easel and had scattered a few painting supplies on an old wooden table, but she hadn't had time to paint since returning from her trip.

"Now that my house is set up, organizing my studio is my next priority."

"What a perfect spot to paint," Anna said, once again admiring the ocean view.

"I can't wait to get started, although I can't do much in the way of marketing my work right now. I don't want anyone to know that I'm in Sand Dune Shores while I'm trying to solve this case. Before he died, John warned me that the man we were looking for was dangerous. The less he knows about me, the better."

"Let's go back to your place and you can fill me in on what you've learned so far."

CHAPTER 2

Anna and Cassie returned next door and settled onto the couch with another mug of hot chocolate.

"Tell me everything," Anna said. "I've been bursting to find out about your trip."

Artie hopped onto Cassie's lap as if he were going to help her tell the story.

"We had quite the trip, Artie and me. First, I went home to Colorado, and I explained to my friends how I lost my memory. Fortunately, they weren't yet worried about me since they knew I was taking an extended trip to Cape Cod. I caught them up on everything I had been through. Then I sorted through my belongings, packed up my house, and informed my landlord that I was moving. I shipped what I wanted to keep and donated the rest. After that, I went to Des Moines to learn more about the art theft that John Seewald served time for. And finally, I attended my brother's wedding in Maine. I just got back last week."

"Considering all you've been through, I'm amazed at how everything worked out," Anna said.

"It truly did. I had been ready for a change for a long time and was contemplating moving to Maine to be near my brother and father before the accident. But I'm glad I landed in Sand Dune Shores. It feels like home."

"So, tell me about Des Moines. Did you make any progress in determining whether John Seewald was innocent?"

"Yes and no. I met with John's former wife, Blaire, his ten-year-old-son, Caleb, and his sister Ellie. I had spoken to Blaire and Ellie on the phone a couple of times, but I wanted to meet them in person. Caleb reminded me so much of John, with the same inquisitive eyes his father had. Our meeting wasn't productive for the case, but I was glad I could answer their questions since I was the last person to see John alive. I assured them he died trying to prove his innocence, and I told them I believed he was innocent as well. I promised to continue the investigation where John had left off and to keep them updated."

"Were they pleased?" Anna asked.

"Ellie and Caleb were, but Blaire seemed skeptical. They divorced eight years ago, and it seemed like she built up a wall."

"That's understandable. She's been through a lot. Her husband went to prison for armed robbery, and she became a single mother overnight. It must have been traumatic for her."

"I know. I think she was afraid of getting Caleb's hopes up, too."

"What makes you so sure that John is innocent?" Anna asked. "When we spoke on the phone, you said you hadn't been in contact with him for years, and then he appeared on your doorstep. How do you know he didn't change during all those years?"

Cassie gazed through the glass door at the waves crashing in the distance. She had asked herself this same question many times, both before she lost her memory and after it returned. "I suppose there is always the chance that he became a different person during the time we didn't see each other. But we were close friends in college, and he even saved my life one time hiking. The John I knew was a caring man and a teacher who lived to inspire young people. I can't sit back and do nothing when there is nobody else working to clear his name. Even if I'm wrong about him, and he does turn out to be guilty, his family deserves answers."

"You're a good friend to him," Anna said.

"Our friendship and my gut instinct aside, there are too many things about this case that don't add up. In addition to visiting Ellie and Blaire, I went to the museum that John was convicted of stealing from. I chatted with an elderly security guard, Norman, who has worked for the museum for over thirty years. He is getting ready to retire, and he told me that John's conviction never sat right with him. He remembered a man with red hair who seemed to be scouting out the museum a few weeks before the robbery."

"What color was John's hair?" Anna asked.

"Brown. But there was no proof that the suspicious man that Norman saw was the same person who robbed the museum."

"But still," Anna said. "The fact that Norman saw someone poking around a couple of weeks before the robbery does indicate that John could be telling the truth. Did the museum have any footage from the night of the robbery?" Anna asked.

"They did, but the robber was dressed in black and wearing a ski mask. However, Norman did say that the robber's body structure matched the red-headed man that he remembers. And there were also pieces stolen from other museums in the area around the same time."

"So, what's your next step?"

"John and I came to Cape Cod because he believed that the painting he was accused of stealing was part of a larger art theft ring. He had a contact who suggested that a man known as Red was involved, and what I learned from Norman indicates that he could be right. John didn't know Red's real name, but he knew he resided somewhere on this part of the Cape."

"John's information does seem consistent with Norman's description of the man he saw a few weeks before the crime," Anna said. "Do you know who John's contact was?"

Cassie shook her head. "I have no idea. I think the best place to start is to follow through on what John and I were planning. Our first goal was to figure out who Red was. That's what we were trying to do before the accident. Then, once we had Red's identity, John hoped we could prove that he framed him. Jake is going to help me try to locate Red."

"I'm looking forward to meeting him. And since Jake is a local, his connections and knowledge of the area will be useful."

"He usually comes to the inn in the evening to visit his parents, so I'm sure we'll see him soon. Speaking of the inn, let's get you settled in."

The women took Anna's car to the *Sand Dune Inn,* even though it was just across the street, so that Anna could unload her suitcase and store her car there. Then Cassie showed her to her room. She left Anna to unpack while she walked Artie and checked in on her employees at the gift shop. Then they met in the lobby at 2:30.

"Are you sure you don't need to spend more time in the gift shop?" Anna asked. "I don't want to keep you away from work."

"No. I only check in periodically with my staff. After I got my memory back, I worked out an arrangement with Elizabeth and Joel. I still manage the shop and do all the hiring, but I don't work the floor unless someone gets sick or needs training. I'm only taking a half-time salary so we can use the other half to hire more part-time help. That way, I'll have enough time to devote to my art. It seemed like a good compromise. I didn't want to abandon them during the tourist season, so we agreed to this arrangement. We're going to reevaluate at the end of the summer."

"That sounds like the perfect compromise," Anna said. "It will be good for you to have a job that puts you in contact with other people. I imagine that painting all day can be lonely."

"Sometimes it can. Although, when I'm in the flow, I love getting lost in my work." Cassie pulled her phone from her pocket and glanced at the time. "You're in for a treat when we eat at the *Sand Dune Tavern,* but it's a little early for dinner. Is there anything in particular you'd like to do now?"

"Why don't we go to Darren's showroom? I wasn't just being polite. I really am looking for a piece of artwork for my mantel."

"Great idea," Cassie said. "I love browsing his creations."

They hopped into Cassie's silver Ford Escape, which she had driven back from Colorado. The SUV, which was practical for the Colorado snow, had a lot of miles on it, so she had been planning to get a new vehicle. Now that she lived by the beach, she was considering a convertible, but that would happen in due time. First, she wanted to settle in before making any more major financial decisions.

They dropped Artie off at the beach house, and within ten minutes, they had arrived at a secluded building with dark brown shingles and white trim. It looked more like a shack than an art showroom.

"I've only been here once," Cassie said. "But I find it so inspiring how he can take something so ordinary, like driftwood, and shape it into something so beautiful. And some of his work is very practical, too."

"It looks like he lives and works here." Anna said, looking up at the apartment on the second floor.

"From what I understand, he is very successful. I'm surprised he hasn't fixed this place up," Cassie said in a soft voice. She didn't want to insult Darren if he was within earshot.

They knocked on the faded blue door to the studio, but nobody answered.

Cassie turned the knob and pushed open the door. "Darren, it's Cassie and Anna."

There was still no answer.

"Maybe he's out back. I'm sure it's okay to go inside since the door is unlocked," Cassie said.

Despite the rough exterior, the showroom was updated on the inside. Though it wasn't large—only about eight hundred square feet—the space felt welcoming. Display tables and shelves lined the walls, with a wooden table against the back wall, beside a door carved with realistic ocean waves. There was another table to the right of the door. The shelves spanned the entire length of the wall, but they paused to frame two windows on either side.

A wide marble table sat in the center of the room, where Darren's driftwood creations were scattered. Sea turtles, fish, birds, and other animals adorned the tables and shelves. There were also frames, wall hangings, and even a section of chairs. A couple of driftwood mantels on the wall particularly caught Cassie's attention.

Anna was immediately drawn to a small seahorse.

"He's beautiful," Cassie said.

"And just the right size for my mantle." She looked at the price tag. "His work really does command a hefty price, but I think I'll go for it. It will be a nice way to commemorate my trip to Sand Dune Shores." She carefully picked up the seahorse. "Let's see if we can find Darren. It looks like there's a room out back. If he's not there, we can go upstairs and see if he's in his apartment. He couldn't have gone far with the door unlocked and all this valuable art inside."

They pushed open a door along the back wall that was slightly ajar. Cassie peeked her head inside and called Darren's name, but he wasn't there.

They came across some boards in the corner with sayings painted on them. One said, "From above, all is clear." Another said, "Nature speaks to those who listen." And a third said, "Sand shifts, but truth remains."

"These are lovely sayings," Anna said. "They have a similar theme."

"I agree. But they look like practice boards. See, the paint is smudged. I wonder if they were commissioned by someone."

"In any case, it doesn't look like he's here. He must have forgotten to lock the door," Anna said.

"We can wait around for a while. We're not in a rush, and he couldn't have gone far."

"There's a staircase on the side of the building that looks like it leads to his residence. I'll see if he's up there. He may have gone upstairs to get something," Anna said.

Anna was heading to the door when Cassie saw half of an arm sticking out from behind the center table on the opposite side of the room from where Anna had found her seahorse. She gasped and jogged over.

Anna turned around. "Are you okay? Why are you running?"

Cassie suddenly stopped and put her hands on her head when she saw the body of the artist with a piece of driftwood carved into a sharp stake and protruding from his chest.

"I found Darren."

CHAPTER 3

Anna almost dropped her driftwood seahorse when she arrived at Darren's body.

Cassie pulled her cell phone from her purse and called 9-1-1. Then, both women inspected the showroom.

Cassie made her way to the large table at the back, which looked like Darren's workstation. It contained a stand, which held a piece of driftwood in place, a steel brush, a couple of different electric sanders, a heat gun, and a wood chisel. Under different circumstances, she would have liked to familiarize herself with his tools, but there was no time for idle curiosity. Rick would be there any minute.

There was a stack of driftwood in a large box behind the table.

"I wonder if the killer made the driftwood stake that was used as the murder weapon here or brought it from elsewhere," Cassie said.

"I suppose it could have happened either way. The killer could have sharpened the stake here or done it somewhere else and brought it here to commit the crime."

"It is ironic that he or she used driftwood as the murder weapon. I wonder if that was intentional, or if the killer just used it because it was available," Cassie said.

"Are you thinking of Maya?"

"That's exactly who I was thinking of."

While they were discussing the pile of wood, a police officer arrived, followed by Detective Rick Blaney a few minutes later. He made a beeline for Cassie, who was now standing by Darren's body.

Rick stopped and stared at the stake protruding from Darren's chest. "Well, that's disturbing."

Cassie introduced Anna and Rick.

"We ran into Darren earlier today while we were walking the beach," Cassie explained. "He offered Anna a discount when she told him she was interested in purchasing a piece of his art. We had some free time before dinner, so we came here so she could browse his work. Since the door was unlocked, we assumed he was somewhere on the premises, so we came inside. Anna chose a driftwood seahorse, and we were looking for him so she could pay for it. That's when we found Darren and called you."

Anna reluctantly handed Rick the seahorse. "I suppose this is part of the crime scene now."

"I'm afraid so." He motioned for her to leave it on the table. "Did you touch anything else in the shop, besides the door and the driftwood seahorse?"

"Just that doorknob when we went out back to search for Darren," Cassie said, pointing to the door that led to the back room.

"You said that you saw Darren earlier on the beach. Did he

say anything unusual? Did he seem nervous or agitated?" Rick asked.

"Not at all," Anna said.

She glanced at Cassie, who nodded in agreement.

"But I didn't know him."

"He seemed cheerful and carefree, just how he always was. We chatted for a few minutes. He was collecting driftwood and..." Cassie paused and glanced at Anna.

"What is it?" Rick asked.

"He was collecting driftwood on the dune by my house, and he was complaining about Maya Deveau giving him a hard time about going onto the dunes."

"She was right," Rick said. "We had to fine him several times over the last few months. I guess he figured it was worth paying the fines to collect his driftwood. We couldn't keep him off that dune. He would just shake his head and insist that he wasn't hurting anything. He said he only wanted to make something meaningful. We couldn't get him to understand that his art didn't give him the right to break the law."

"Judging from the price of his art, it was probably worth paying the fines so that he could craft more art," Anna said.

"That may have been part of the problem," Rick said.

"Did you say that Maya lives on the beach?" Anna asked.

"Yes. She lives in one of the larger homes on the other side of the public entrance from mine. I'm pretty sure she is able to see the dune from her house," Cassie said.

"Maybe she saw Darren collecting wood today and decided she'd had enough."

"That's possible," Rick said.

Two crime scene technicians entered the showroom and

Rick gave them a curt wave. "I know where to find you ladies if I have any more questions. You're free to go."

The women started toward the door, but Rick interrupted them. "Is this by chance the same Anna you stayed with in Seagull Cove just after your accident?"

Anna nodded. "That's me. When Cassie called and told me that her memory returned, I had to come in person to see her. It looks like everything worked out for the best."

"We gave our Cassie a tough time when she first arrived," Rick said. "It took me a while to trust her."

"All is forgiven, Rick. I'm just glad the last couple of months are behind me and I am finally moving forward with my life."

After leaving Darren's showroom, the women returned to the inn and settled onto the brown leather sofas in the library, near the stone fireplace.

After a few minutes, Cassie broke the silence. "I think I'm still trying to process what just happened."

"I know what you mean. After a relaxing walk on the beach and checking into this beautiful inn, seeing poor Darren with that horrible stake through his heart took the wind out of my sails."

"I'm afraid I'll never look at a piece of driftwood the same again," Cassie said.

"Maybe it's better I didn't get that seahorse."

"You're probably right."

"What should we do now?" Anna asked. "I'm not in the mood to play tourist this afternoon."

"Me, either."

"Did you say that Maya Deveau lives nearby?"

"Yeah. She lives a few houses down from me. It's a short walk from here. Are you thinking what I'm thinking?"

"I'm only here for a few days, but we could interview a few people before I leave."

"We kind of owe it to Darren," Cassie said. "As far as we know, we were the last people to see him alive, besides the killer."

"It's like déjà vu from your trip to Seagull Cove."

"Looks like the sleuthing team is back together," Cassie said.

"But this time, you're the one with the local connections and I'm *your* sidekick."

Cassie chuckled. "I guess you're right. I'm not sure how I feel about that."

"Let's try to talk to Maya before dinner. I need some more time before my appetite comes back, anyway."

CHAPTER 4

Cassie and Anna turned left from Starboard Lane onto Cranberry Avenue, arriving at Maya's house. Her two-story tan house with white trim was just beyond the public entrance to the beach.

Anna craned her neck to see the windows. "Maya could definitely see the sand dune from several of her windows."

"Remember how Darren was looking over his shoulder when we first saw him? Maybe he knew Maya was watching him," Cassie said.

"It's possible, if he passed this way to get to the beach. Is there another access point where Darren could have entered?"

"This is the only legal one, but he could have cut through someone's private property. Judging from how often he climbed the dunes, we do know that he liked to disregard rules," Cassie said. "I suppose he could have a friend who lives on the beach and gave him permission to cut through their yard, but I tend to think he didn't. I've seen him using public access many times."

"In that case, he was probably looking over his shoulder

because he knew that Maya was watching him from her window."

"I keep replaying our conversation with him in my mind, and I can't think of anything he said that gave me the impression he felt he was in danger," Anna said.

"I agree. He seemed more like a child trying to get away with something than someone who felt threatened. There was a playfulness about him."

Cassie pressed Maya's doorbell, and within a few minutes a woman with dark brown, shoulder length hair, who looked to be in her forties, opened the door.

"Can I help you?" she asked. Her gaze stopped on Cassie. "I've seen you walking along the beach. You're new to the neighborhood, aren't you?"

"Yes. I don't believe we've met in person. I'm Cassie and this is my friend, Anna. I work at the *Sand Dune Inn*."

"Nice to meet you both. Maya Deveau," she said, extending her hand.

"Would it be okay if we came in for a few minutes? We had a question, and we thought you might be able to help us."

"Sure," she said, stepping back so they could enter. "If it has anything to do with this neighborhood, I'm your girl."

They followed Maya into the living room. The house had a similar layout to Cassie's, except the kitchen and living space were twice as large, and instead of three bedrooms on the left, there was one room and a staircase. But it had the same amazing ocean view.

"You have a beautiful home," Anna said.

She smiled broadly. "Thank you."

Cassie noticed a pair of binoculars on the coffee table. She glanced at Anna, who also saw them.

"I'm sorry that I haven't come over to welcome you to the neighborhood," Maya said. "I've been very busy."

Cassie wondered if by busy, she meant planning a murder.

"That's alright. I just returned from a road trip, anyway, so I haven't been home much since I purchased the beach house."

"I hear that you'll be living there full time. I was so happy to hear that. Our beach is overrun with tourists already. We don't need more seasonal rentals." She paused and furrowed her brow. "Are you roommates? I thought you were living alone."

Cassie felt torn. She felt violated that Maya knew so much about her life without ever having met her. But on the other hand, she was pleased that Maya was talkative. Her gossipy nature would work to their advantage.

The women shook their heads.

"I'm just visiting for a few days," Anna said.

"We stopped by because we were wondering if you heard the news," Cassie said.

"You'll have to be a little more specific," Maya said with an amused laugh.

"It's about Darren Germain."

Her smile disappeared as she appeared to be gathering her thoughts. "Has he been causing problems again? He's always poking around in that dune near your house with no regard for the fragile landscape, only to gather driftwood for his own selfish purposes. You wouldn't believe what he charges for those monstrosities. I'll bet he was carrying an armful of driftwood."

Cassie guessed she already knew that, but she humored Maya. "He was. He marched right past one of those signs that say, 'Stay off the Dunes,'" she said, hoping to gain Maya's trust.

Maya perked up, apparently believing she had found a sympathetic ear. "If you just moved here, you don't even know the half of it. This time of year, he's always trying to stock up on driftwood so he can gouge tourists with those hideous pieces. And this isn't the only beach where he scavenges. He goes up and down the coast, trampling on sand dunes, no doubt."

"How do you know that?"

"He'd have to with all the driftwood he uses. Plus, I'm head of the *Sandy Shores Preservation*, a local conservation group. I hear things from other people. Anyway, what's old Darren up to these days?"

"He was murdered this afternoon," Cassie blurted out, looking Maya straight in the eyes to gauge her reaction.

Her eyes widened, but it was hard to tell whether her shock was genuine.

"You're kidding me," she said. She sounded as if she had just received a juicy piece of gossip rather than learning that a man had passed. "Great. I'll probably be a suspect. Just what I need."

Cassie tried to hide her disgust at the woman's less-than-sympathetic reaction to a man's violent death.

"I wonder who he ticked off enough to provoke murder," Maya said.

"We were wondering the same thing," Cassie said.

"I certainly hope people don't think that *I* did it," she said, putting her hand on her chest. "You don't think they'll say that, do you?"

"Not if you have an alibi," Cassie said.

"Good thinking. You said he was murdered this afternoon?" Maya asked.

"It had to be between 1:00 and 2:30. We saw him walking the beach around 1:00, and his body was discovered a little after 2:30."

"That's unfortunate. I was here in my house alone between those hours, so I don't have an alibi. I'm sure it's only a matter of time before the police come knocking on my door. Thanks for the heads up."

Cassie was surprised that Maya assumed that because they happened to live a few houses apart, she would protect her. But she decided to let Maya believe that.

"I suppose I should treat his death with a little more respect," Maya said. "At least he died in his studio. He did love making that driftwood art, so he was in his happy place."

Cassie searched her mind to try to remember if they had mentioned that piece of information.

"How did you know where he died?" Anna asked, apparently noticing the same thing.

Maya's eyes widened. "I didn't know that, but I assumed it was the case, because you said he was collecting driftwood this afternoon. He probably brought it straight back to his studio afterwards."

"You didn't seem surprised to learn that someone had it out for Darren. What made you feel that way?" Cassie asked. "Did he have a lot of enemies?"

"He only moved to town a couple of years ago, but he certainly has managed to ruffle a lot of feathers."

"Is there anyone in particular who comes to mind?" Anna asked.

Maya narrowed her eyes. "There are a couple of people." She leaned forward. "Lena Heins, for one."

"Who's Lena?" Cassie asked.

"She's a local artist and one of several people who were unhappy with his rapid success. I once heard her call him a scavenger rather than an artist."

"It sounds like she was jealous," Cassie said.

"I think she was. I didn't mind that Darren was rough around the edges. It's no secret that I wasn't a fan of his art, but a lot of people were. My issue with him was that he didn't take care of the environment. Some of us work very hard to preserve the natural beauty of Sand Dune Shores. An outsider had no right to come in and disrespect that."

"That's a fair point," Anna said. "I'm sure the fact that he made a lot of money from his art didn't help."

"That's exactly right. That's what I meant when I said that I wasn't surprised he got himself murdered. For a man who was earning a living from our local resources, he had a flippant attitude about the environment. But I had a plan to fix that."

"What kind of plan?" Cassie asked.

"I managed to convince Lena to give Darren some competition. She's a sculptor, so I figured she could make driftwood art just as well as Darren. And maybe if she could cut into his business, he would relocate to another town." Maya shrugged. "It was worth a shot, anyway. I even collected some wood along the beach and delivered it to her garage to encourage her. And it worked. That's when I figured out that Lena's problem with Darren wasn't his art, but that she was jealous of a newcomer's quick success. She's been working in a coffee shop for the past seven years trying to get her career off the ground."

"So, you're thinking she may have decided to speed up her success by killing Darren?"

Maya shrugged. "Maybe she figured if she could eliminate

the competition, she could take over his customers and become a full-time artist."

"Is there anyone else you can think of who held a grudge against him?" Cassie asked.

"Hmm… let me think. There's Chet Mercer. From what I hear, he's always been suspicious of Darren. When Darren came to town, he had nothing. He never talked about his past. If anyone brought it up, he would change the subject. Then he became extremely successful very fast. He spent a lot of money renovating his studio and he got a fancy pickup truck to haul that wood. Chet was convinced that Darren's art alone was not enough to bring that level of financial success. He believed Darren was into something shady."

"Like what?"

"You'd have to ask Chet. I think he felt that Darren was taking customers away from more established businesses. Chet supported my idea for Lena to give Darren some competition, but maybe he felt the plan was too slow."

"That doesn't sound like a motive for murder," Anna said.

"You don't know Chet. He grew up in town and is very protective of the local economy. He's president of the Chamber of Commerce, and his father was before him. He tried to convince Darren that he would do better in a state that has a longer summer, such as the Carolinas, but Darren made it clear he was here to stay."

Maya's phone pinged with a text.

"If you ask me—and you did, mind you—I think he would have done anything to get Darren out of town," she continued.

Her phone pinged for a second time, followed by a third.

She picked her phone up from the coffee table and glanced at the screen. "Word is spreading about Darren's death." Her phone rang, and Maya suddenly looked bored with their conversation. "Please excuse me. I should get that..." She tapped on her screen and put the phone to her ear. "Margaret, did you hear what happened to Darren?" She shook her head. "I know. I'll bet I'll be the first suspect. It seems Darren is still causing me problems, even in death."

Since Maya was clearly done with them, Cassie and Anna showed themselves out and walked back to the inn.

CHAPTER 5

"That was a strange conversation," Anna said as they walked back to the *Sand Dune Inn*.

"I know. And kind of disturbing. Maya completely assumed that we were there to warn her. It didn't occur to her that we thought of her as a suspect."

"I suppose she figured you were just coming over to introduce yourself after moving to the neighborhood and to gossip a bit. Maybe that caused her to lower her guard. She clearly doesn't know about the other cases you've solved," Anna said.

"Not only was her reaction cold, but she knew that he died in his studio. I suppose she could have assumed that was the case because he had been collecting driftwood, but there could be more to it," Cassie said.

"I agree," Anna said. "That was a big assumption. It could have easily happened on his way home, or he could have been lured somewhere else by the killer."

"Or he could have gone to another beach to collect more wood, or anywhere else, for that matter. He owned a pickup truck with plenty of room, so he didn't need to go straight home. The fact that Maya knew he was murdered in his studio is a red flag," Cassie said.

"She could have watched him leave the beach, and followed him to his studio."

"We should talk to Lena and Chet next," Cassie said. "I've met both of them at the inn. Elizabeth introduced me to Lena once, since we're both artists. And she introduced me to Chet, because she thought it would be good for me to meet the head of the Chamber of Commerce—both in connection with the inn and as an artist. He's a realtor, but she mentioned that he also invests in a lot of local businesses."

"I can see why he wouldn't want someone like Darren to succeed," Anna said. "It could compromise his investments, and if he has a lot of history in this town, he might prefer that other businesses thrive. Like the businesses of his friends."

"Maya mentioned that Lena works in a coffee shop. Jake might know which one."

"Sounds like a plan. In the meantime, my appetite is returning," Anna said.

"Same. Let's have dinner at the *Sand Dune Tavern*. You're in for a treat."

Since it was a Monday evening, the tavern wasn't busy. They decided to order an array of appetizers to share, so Cassie went out back and placed their order with the chef. When she returned, Jake was sitting with Anna.

"I saw the two of you walk in, so I thought I'd come over and say hello," Jake said. "Anna was just telling me about your afternoon."

"Did you know Darren?" Cassie asked.

"Everyone did—at least everyone knew of him. His presence in town was controversial. A small town like Sand Dune

Shores isn't big on newcomers moving in and taking business from the locals. But nobody has ever gotten murdered for it before."

"Maybe there's a different reason he was killed," Cassie said.

"Anything's possible," Jake said. "He did march to the beat of a different drum."

"What do you mean?" Anna asked.

"Well, he was very secretive about his plans when he first moved to town. Then one day he opened a small showroom, and his driftwood art immediately became a huge hit. Some people were angry that he trespassed on the sand dune across the street, and his attitude didn't help. He seemed to think he was justified because he was using it to create art."

"He obviously made at least one enemy who was angry enough to kill him," Anna said.

"Can you join us for dinner?" Cassie asked.

"I wish I could, but I promised my parents I'd eat with them. I do have a few minutes for coffee, though."

Rob, the server, was dropping off drinks at the next table.

"I'll grab you that coffee, Jake," he said.

Jake smiled. "Thanks."

"Can I get you anything, Heather?"

Cassie smirked. "No, thanks."

He started to walk away, then stopped and turned abruptly. "Sorry, Cassie," he said with an apologetic smile. "I'm still trying to get used to your real name. None of us can believe all that you were going through during the past couple of months. Although it does explain why you never liked to talk about your past."

"Because she couldn't remember it," Jake said.

"I'm sorry about your memory loss, but I'm glad it led to you staying in town."

"Thanks, Rob. So am I."

Jake beamed at Cassie's response, and Anna seemed to pick up on his reaction.

Rob returned with Jake's coffee, and he savored the first sip. "I needed this. It's been so busy at my store, and it's only May."

"Jake owns a recreation shop where tourists can rent paddleboards, kayaks, bikes—basically anything they need to enjoy the outdoors," Cassie said.

"Sounds like a fun way to make a living," Anna said.

Cassie chuckled. "Says the woman who owns an ice cream shop."

Jake laughed. "I would never fit in my clothes if I owned an ice cream shop."

"The struggle is real," Anna said.

"With everything that happened today, have you had a chance to fill Anna in on John Seewald and our investigation there?" Jake asked.

"I caught her up to speed this afternoon when we spent some time at my beach house."

"I'm glad you're helping her," Anna said. "It's good that she has someone on her side who knows the whole story, not to mention someone who is familiar with the area. Cassie tells me that your first step in figuring out Red's identity is to talk to someone in the art world about some local art thefts."

"Yes. Her name is Trudy. She's been a family friend since before I was born."

"It seems like a good place to start," Anna said.

"You just name the day," Jake said to Cassie. "We can wait until Anna leaves so you can spend more time together."

"Don't put it off on my account. There are plenty of things I can do to occupy myself. You don't have to babysit me. Actually, I might rent one of Jake's bikes. I'd love to get some physical activity while I'm here."

"In that case, I could break away for a while in the late afternoon tomorrow," Jake said. "I'll give Trudy a call and see if she could spare some time then."

"Great," Cassie said. "Text me and let me know."

"I will." He took another long sip of coffee. "So, am I correct in assuming that the two of you will be looking into Darren's murder?"

"I'm not sure how much time we'll have since Anna is only here for a few days, but we did speak with Maya Deveau this afternoon," Cassie said.

"That seems like a good place to start. She was always on Darren about collecting driftwood from the dunes."

"She's still on the list," Cassie said. "She somehow knew that Darren was murdered in his studio, even though that's not public knowledge yet."

"That's interesting. Do you have any other suspects?"

"Maya pointed the finger at an artist named Lena Heins and a local businessman, Chet Mercer."

"I can see Chet. He is very protective of the local businesses. But why Lena?" Jake asked.

"According to Maya, she was jealous of Darren's success," Anna said.

"And resentful, too," Cassie added.

"Well, I believe Trudy has worked with Lena. You could

see what she thinks about her character while we're there talking to her about the other case."

"Great tip. Thanks, Jake," Cassie said.

"Do you know how we could reach Chet?" Anna asked Jake.

"He owns a vacation rental company on Route 28. They're super busy this time of year, so he's usually in the office. It's called *Beachside Vacations*."

"Perfect. Thanks," Anna said.

"And how about Lena?" Cassie asked. "Do you know what coffee shop she works in?"

"I'm not sure, but I'll ask Trudy when I call her." Jake emptied the rest of his coffee cup with one long sip and stood up. "I'd better get going. I'll call Trudy tonight and text you tomorrow. Nice meeting you, Anna. Maybe I'll see you at the shop."

"I'm sure you will."

"He seems sweet," Anna said after he left.

"He is. And he's been a good friend."

"I could be wrong, but I had the impression he's interested in more than friendship."

"Now that I have my memory back and have decided to settle in Sand Dune Shores, things seem to be moving in that direction," Cassie said. "But I'm okay with a slower pace. There's been a lot of change in my life lately."

"I understand. But for what it's worth, I get a good vibe from him," Anna said.

"You're a good judge of character, so that's good to hear."

"Hopefully, you can get some more information about Lena when you talk with Trudy. In the meantime, should we spin by Chet's office in the morning?" Anna asked.

"I think we should."

Once they finished their dinner, Anna yawned.

"That's my cue to give you some time alone. You had a long drive earlier, not to mention a long day since you arrived. I have to walk Artie anyway. Would you like to meet here at 9:00?"

"Sounds great. See you then."

CHAPTER 6

Cassie drove her car home and took Artie for a brisk walk to burn off some of that puppy energy. Later that evening, Jake texted to confirm that Trudy was available to speak with them at her art gallery the following day at 3:00. He also sent the name of the coffee shop where Lena worked: *Bobbi's Brews.*

The following morning, Cassie arrived at the gift shop just before opening time at 9:00. Beginning on May 1, the gift shop was back to its summer hours, which meant it was open from 9 AM to 7 PM. With Memorial Day weekend just a few days away, everyone was gearing up for the summer.

She helped her employees open the shop so she could check in with one of her new hires. She had hired four college students—Sierra, Kayla, Tyler, and Eli—so she scheduled them with Leslie and Monica, her more experienced employees.

After chatting with Monica and Sierra for a while, she left Artie with them and went to the tavern to enjoy a hearty breakfast with Anna. Artie had become a fixture in the gift shop, and the staff and customers had grown accustomed to seeing him there. She was grateful that she could leave him there when she needed to.

"Do you eat like this every morning?" Anna asked, looking wide-eyed at the French toast, eggs, and bacon in front of her.

"Are you kidding? I wish! I only splurge once in a while. But since you're here, it feels like I'm on vacation, too."

While they ate, Anna caught Cassie up on the people she met during her stay in Seagull Cove. After breakfast, they enjoyed a second cup of coffee, and Cassie took their dishes to the kitchen.

"Shall we head to Chet's real estate office?" Anna asked.

"Let's do it. I've been meaning to find out what my second unit could command for rent during the summer months, so it will be a good excuse to talk to him."

They hopped into Cassie's silver Ford Escape, and she punched the address into her GPS. A few minutes later, they parked in front of *Beachside Vacations*, which was located in a busy strip mall.

Cassie glanced at the listings posted in the window on the way in. "Sydney told me I could charge a lot of money for the unit that I'm currently using as my art studio, but I had no idea she meant *this* much."

The women entered the lobby of the rental office, which was bustling with activity. A woman stood up from behind one of six cubicles and greeted them with a friendly smile. "How can I help you?"

"A friend recommended we talk with Chet Mercer. Is he available?"

Her shoulders dropped, which Cassie assumed was

because she believed she had missed out on a commission. "Sure. I'll get him."

A couple of minutes later, a man with blond wavy hair and an athletic build popped out of his cubicle. "Hello, ladies. I'm Chet Mercer. How can I help you today?"

"I was looking for some general information on potentially renting out my beach house," Cassie explained. She left out the fact that she was only considering it for the future.

"You've come to the right place. Why don't we sit down and talk?" He led them to a cubicle in the back, where there was a desk with a laptop computer and two chairs facing the desk. He spun his chair around to face the women.

Cassie pulled her phone from her pocket and showed Chet some photos of her second unit. "I recently moved to town and bought this duplex. I live in one of the units, but I was wondering how much I could charge for the second one if I chose to rent it out during the high season."

"Welcome to Sand Dune Shores," he said as he took Cassie's phone and scrolled through the photos. "This is a great unit. It's a bit on the rustic side, but the location is phenomenal."

"It has three small bedrooms, one bathroom, and is located directly on the beach."

"Judging from what other similar units have been getting this summer, I think I could get about $4,000 per week for it. Minus our fee, of course."

Cassie looked at Anna, who seemed equally surprised as she was.

"That's more than I thought. I'll definitely consider it," Cassie said.

Chet handed her a business card. "Let me know what you decide. I'll take good care of you."

"Will do." Cassie stood, pretending to leave, before broaching the subject they really came to discuss. "I'd want to be careful who I rent to. You must hear about all sorts of local drama. You won't rent it to anyone unsafe, will you?"

"What do you mean?" Chet asked.

Cassie sat down again. "Did you hear what happened to Darren Germain? Apparently, there's a killer on the loose in Sand Dune Shores."

"Darren was actually on Cassie's beach the day he died," Anna said. "We talked to him for a few minutes while we were taking a walk."

The women left out that they found his body later the same afternoon.

"Let me guess. He was collecting driftwood. And probably from the sand dune, where he shouldn't be." He put on a frown that Cassie wasn't convinced was sincere. "I heard about his death. But you don't have to worry about that. I'm sure it wasn't a random murder. Besides, we do a background check on all of our renters."

"That's a relief," Cassie said.

"Did you know Darren?" Anna asked.

"Sure. He had only been in town for a couple of years, but everyone knew him because of his driftwood art."

"From what we heard, his presence brought a lot of controversy."

Chet raised his eyebrows.

"I work at the *Sand Dune Inn,* and people like to gossip there."

"I see. I suppose you could say that his presence in town

was controversial. Let's just say that the local environmentalists weren't happy about the way he would comb the beaches to collect driftwood, and some of the local businesses were jealous of his quick success."

"I heard that one of my neighbors used to call the police whenever he was on the dunes, which led to him being slapped with a few fines."

"That was probably Maya Deveau. As head of the Chamber of Commerce, she would regularly keep me informed of his activities. She wanted me to throw him out of the Chamber of Commerce because of what she called 'destructive business practices,' but I didn't really have grounds to do that."

"You mentioned that there was jealousy among local business owners over his quick success," Cassie said.

"That's true, but I can't imagine anyone would kill him over that."

"Just between us, who do you think did it?" Anna asked.

He lowered his voice. "I spoke with the police last night and it seems like he had a lot of enemies, so it's hard to say. But if I can offer you some advice, I wouldn't go poking around that hornet's nest. You could end up getting hurt. His enemies are obviously more dangerous than anyone realized. You should stay far away from it." He averted his gaze.

Cassie studied Chet. "You have a theory, don't you?"

He let out a deep breath. "Let's just say that I was keeping an eye on the guy. I don't trust the prices he commanded for his art."

"It seems that people were willing to pay those prices, though," Cassie said. "I've seen some of his pieces. They took a lot of skill and time to create."

"Perhaps. But I've seen similar businesses fail over the

years. I don't think there's as much of a market for it in Sand Dune Shores as he made it seem."

"I don't understand," Cassie said. "How else could he have been so successful?"

"That's a very good question," Chet said.

"Are you implying he was making his money in some other way?" Anna asked.

"I'm not saying he was, but it would make sense. I keep my finger on the pulse of the local business community. It doesn't add up that he made so much money so quickly. I'm not trying to gossip, mind you. I just want you to feel safe if you should decide to rent out your beach house. As I said, I doubt Darren's murder was random. I think it's possible that he was involved in something shady."

"Are you saying that you think his driftwood business was a front for something else?" Cassie asked. "Do you mean like laundering money?"

Chet's phone rang.

"I'm only telling you what I told the police. I wouldn't rule it out. I've got to take this call, but I mean it. You should leave the investigating to the police and don't worry about renters not being safe. None of our clients have ever had a problem like that."

They hopped back into Cassie's SUV. "I wish we had time to ask him about an alibi," Cassie said, pulling onto Route 28.

"I know. And I'm not sure if that was a genuine warning or a threat," Anna said.

"I agree. It was hard to tell. But whatever the reason, he was trying to steer us away from investigating."

"You're an artist. Do you think there was a market for his work in Sand Dune Shores?" Anna asked.

"Driftwood is making a comeback in art and in home decorating. I'm not sure why Chet would have said that."

"So, it seems like we're dealing with three possible motives," Anna said.

"Right. Either Darren was genuinely successful, and somebody got jealous, an environmentalist decided to take matters into his or her own hands, or Darren was involved with something illegal that got him killed."

"It seems that way," Cassie said. "We need to keep digging. Maybe we'll learn more when we talk to Lena."

CHAPTER 7

When Cassie and Anna returned to the *Sand Dune Inn*, there was a teal and white ten-speed bicycle in the corner of the foyer. An envelope with Anna's name was taped to the front.

Anna opened it and discovered that it contained a local trail map and a note that read, 'Enjoy! Jake.'

"That was so thoughtful of him. He's a keeper," Anna said, winking at Cassie.

Cassie smiled. "It's a perfect day for a bike ride. You should take advantage of the beautiful weather. I need to take care of a few things in the gift shop, and then I can work on setting up my studio until the meeting with Trudy later this afternoon."

"Don't forget to find out what you can about Lena," Anna said.

"I won't forget. How about if I come to the inn after, and we can have dinner together?"

"That sounds perfect. I'll see you back here when you're finished."

Anna changed, then took off with her bike while Cassie spent some time taking inventory and placing orders. The painted sand dollars that she had been making continued to do well, so she ordered more supplies. Then she took Artie, who had been hanging out in the shop, for a long walk and returned to her studio to do some organizing. She texted Jake to let him know where she was, and before she knew it, it was 2:30, and he was knocking at the door of her studio.

Artie gave him the usual enthusiastic greeting.

"I haven't been in here since you moved in," he said. "This is perfect for a studio. Not to mention that it will be easy to sneak away in the summer for a swim or a paddle when you need a break from painting. I can hook you up with some used kayaks if you'd like. I'll be getting rid of some inventory soon."

"I just might take you up on that. I was thinking of getting a couple of kayaks—one for me, and one in case I want to paddle with a friend. I think they'd fit under the porch."

"That would be perfect. I can store them for you at my shop in the winter if you don't have a spot for them."

Cassie scanned her studio. "Or better yet, I could hang them on the walls."

"Sweet idea. Come by the shop whenever you're ready and I'll show you what I have."

Jake admired the paintings she had hung on her walls. "We have to get this case solved so you can start exhibiting and selling your work. I hate that you're still in limbo."

"Agreed. But it's worth it to give John's family some answers."

"On that note, let's get going."

They hopped into Jake's grey Jeep Wrangler and drove to a

small art gallery the next town over, where a few tourists were milling about and admiring the artwork.

An elegant woman who looked to be in her early sixties came out from behind a desk to greet them.

"Hi, Aunt Trudy," Jake said, kissing her on the cheek.

"Hi, sweetie. I was surprised to receive your call. It's always wonderful to see you."

"This is Cassie, the woman I was telling you about."

"Hello, Cassie. Jake and his parents speak very highly of you."

Cassie perused a few of the paintings displayed in the gallery and felt a surge of inspiration. "You have some beautiful pieces."

"Cassie is a talented artist. One of her paintings is in the foyer of the inn," Jake said. "And she's been painting beach scenes on sand dollars, which have been a huge hit at the gift shop."

Trudy narrowed her brow. "I remember seeing that painting the last time I visited your parents. I noticed they had replaced the other one. Jake's right. You have a wonderful eye. I'd love to see more of your work."

"I'd love to show you some when I'm ready to start pitching it to galleries."

Trudy raised an eyebrow. "Usually, people respond more eagerly when a gallery owner offers to look at their work."

"It's kind of a long story," Jake said. He glanced around. "Could we speak in your office?"

"Of course. Veronica can keep an eye on things out front."

They followed Trudy to a small office behind the showroom, and Jake closed the door behind them.

"Your message was very cryptic. I have to admit, I'm curious about all the secrecy."

"First, you have to promise not to breathe a word about what we're about to tell you to anyone," Jake said.

"Of course. You know that I can keep a secret." Trudy smirked at Jake, who laughed and shook his head.

"I'm never going to live that down, am I?" he asked.

"Probably not. But I never did breathe a word to your parents."

Jake blushed and glanced at Cassie. "Let's just say Aunt Trudy got me out of a tight spot when I was a teenager. My parents were out of town, and I threw a party that got out of hand. When I lost control of it, I called Aunt Trudy. She shut it down and helped me calm down. I was so scared that I never tried it again. She remained true to her word and never told my parents."

"Everyone needs an aunt like that," Cassie said.

"Jake had clearly learned his lesson, so I didn't see any reason to tell Elizabeth and Joel. We got the place cleaned up in a jiffy and they were never the wiser."

"That's a sweet story, but unfortunately, the stakes are a little higher on this secret," Cassie said.

"Why don't you start at the beginning?" Trudy said.

They told Trudy the whole story—how Cassie lost her memory while traveling with John Seewald, that he was a recent ex-convict, and that he passed away in the accident that temporarily took her memory. She recounted how once her memory returned, she remembered that she had been on Cape Cod trying to help John prove his innocence. She also told Trudy about her conversation with the security guard about Red.

"Wow, you have been on quite the journey in the past couple of months. And you started a job at the inn and bought a home in Sand Dune Shores in the midst of all this?"

"It's been a whirlwind," Cassie said.

"That explains why I could have sworn the woman the Hardings hired to run the gift shop was named Heather."

"That was the name I was using, since I didn't know my real one."

"So, you believe this John Seewald was falsely convicted of art theft," Trudy said.

"I think so. We were close friends as young adults, but we had been out of touch for many years before he popped back into my life. So, there's always the chance that he could have changed. But I didn't have that impression. He wanted to clear his name for his young son, Caleb. I'd like to solve this case and find out one way or another, even if I'm wrong about his innocence."

"Cassie has a knack for solving crimes," Jake said. "She worked as a police sketch artist back in Colorado, and she has helped to solve several murders since moving to Sand Dune Shores. If anyone can figure out what happened, she can."

"If John was right, then this man called Red resides in the area. Our first step is to figure out who he is," Cassie said. "We need to know his identity before we can even try to prove his guilt."

"Your friend John may have been right."

"What makes you say that?" Cassie asked.

"There have been an unusual amount of art thefts in the area in the past five years. In fact, I was recently discussing it with some colleagues because there is growing concern. A gallery about a half hour away in Dennis Port recently had one. The thief was never caught, but the owner is a good friend. It's going to take her a long time to recover financially from it."

"I'm so sorry to hear that. Did she mention any other details?"

Trudy paused as if reflecting. "I don't think so, but I wasn't focused on the details because I was trying to comfort my friend. All I remember is that she had received some expensive art just before the break-in. It was as if the thief knew when to come. She thinks he or she cased the joint a couple of weeks before, because her staff reported seeing someone suspicious. They didn't realize it at the time, but only in hindsight, after the theft. When they looked at the security footage, there was nothing. The camera..."

Cassie completed her sentence. "The camera tapes over the old footage after twenty-four hours."

"Exactly. So, if someone comes in to scope the place out, by the time there's a robbery, the footage of the suspicious person is gone."

"That's exactly what happened in Des Moines, too."

"I've been keeping an eye out for anyone suspicious since the thief might target another gallery next. Several of us have pieces from that same artist. We're hoping the thief realizes we're on high alert and decides not to strike again in this area."

"We don't mean to worry you, Aunt Trudy, but is there any way you can beef up your security?"

"I could hire a night guard, but that would be expensive. The police are aware of the situation, and they are driving by at random times. The local media covered the heightened police security, so with any luck the thief already knows not to try anything."

"Hopefully, that will be enough to deter them," Jake said.

"You two be careful. This sounds like a dangerous situation. In the meantime, I'll keep my ears open and put out some feelers to see if anyone knows anything."

"We promise we'll be careful," Jake said.

"Before we go, I have a question on another matter that you might be able to help with. My friend Anna and I are the ones who found the body of Darren Germain."

"Oh, my goodness, how awful! I heard about Darren's death. It seems the local art community is undergoing a lot of trials lately."

"This was particularly gruesome because he was killed with a piece of driftwood."

Trudy's eyes widened. "Oh, my."

"Darren was relatively new to town, so it's looking like the killer is either another artist who was jealous of his success, or an environmentalist who was upset because he would sometimes take driftwood from restricted areas."

"I sure hope it wasn't another artist. This community doesn't need that kind of bad publicity."

"I was wondering if you knew Lena Heins. I heard she was one of the artists who was particularly envious of Darren's success. Do you know anything about her?"

"I do know her," Trudy said. "She struck me as someone who feels entitled to success. But she's young. Hopefully, she'll learn to be more supportive of other artists. The strange thing is, she openly criticized Darren's work, insisting it wasn't real art. Yet, a friend of mine saw her collecting driftwood on the beach. Seems like she was planning to compete with him after all."

"That's what I heard, too."

"That's strange," Jake said.

"My friend thought so, too, which is why she mentioned it to me. At the time, I thought it was good. I thought she was becoming more respectful of other artists and diversifying herself. She is a talented sculptor, so I think she'd be good at it."

"It also means she would have had the tools and the driftwood to commit the crime," Cassie said.

The color drained from Trudy's face. "I hadn't thought of that."

"It sounds like we need to keep her on our list of suspects," Cassie said.

CHAPTER 8

After their conversation with Trudy, Cassie and Jake drove back to the inn.

"I didn't realize there had been so many art thefts in the area over the past five years," Jake said.

"Thank you for introducing me to Trudy. She could be a valuable resource."

"She said she'd keep her ears open. Maybe she'll learn something from one of her colleagues. She's a good person to have in the loop."

It was 4:00 when they returned to the inn, and Anna was just getting back from her bike ride.

"I can't thank you enough for loaning me the bike today," Anna said, taking off her helmet and revealing her sunkissed cheeks. "I found a long, winding path through the woods and I followed it all afternoon."

"My pleasure," Jake said. He took the bike from Anna. "I'll throw it in my trunk now. I'm headed back to the shop, anyway."

He loaded the bike into his trunk and drove away.

"I'm anxious to hear about your conversation with Trudy, but I should take a shower first," Anna said.

"How about we meet at the tavern in an hour?"

"Perfect. I worked up a hearty appetite. I'll see you then."

Cassie stopped in the gift shop to check in on her staff and to pick up Artie. Then she took the puppy for another walk.

Sydney called while she was walking. "I wanted to be sure to have you and Anna over before she leaves for Seagull Cove. When does she go home?"

"Thursday evening."

"Wow. That was a quick visit. In that case, I'm glad I called. Can you come over for dinner tomorrow evening?"

"I don't see why not. I'll double check with Anna tonight and let you know."

"Perfect. By the way, I heard about what happened to Darren Germain. I assume that you two are investigating."

"Anna and I took a walk along the beach with Artie after you left yesterday, and we ran into Darren. He was collecting driftwood."

"Let me guess. He was on the dunes, completely ignoring the signs that say, 'Stay off the Dunes.'"

"You got it."

"I saw him doing that a lot when I lived in the beach house."

"That's not all. He offered Anna a discount on a piece of his driftwood art, so we went to his studio so she could choose something."

"Don't tell me that you…"

"Yup. We discovered his body. Someone had sharpened a piece of driftwood into a stake and stabbed him with it."

Sydney gasped. "You're kidding me. Poor Darren. It

sounds like the killer was trying to send some sort of sick message."

"Anna and I had the same thought. Why else would they have used driftwood as the murder weapon? It was like some sort of twisted poetic justice."

"You should talk to Maya Deveau. She lives a few doors down from you and when I lived in your beach house, she was forever bending my ear about Darren."

"We already did. She's on our list of suspects. Do you think Maya was angry enough to kill him?"

"She's very passionate about the sand dunes. I wouldn't rule her out."

"Thanks, Sydney. I'll text you tonight to confirm dinner."

Cassie took Artie on an extra long walk, since she was going to leave him alone again while she ate at the tavern. Then she fed him, played with him for a few minutes, and walked across the street to meet Anna.

The women sat at a corner table where they could speak privately, and Cassie ran back into the kitchen to place their order. Anna chose a chicken and pasta dish, and Cassie ordered shrimp on a skewer with rice. While they ate, Cassie caught Anna up on her conversation with Trudy.

"It sounds like you are moving in the right direction," Anna said. "If John Seewald believed the real thief lived in this area, and there's been an uptick in thefts, then he may have been right. The robbery in Des Moines eight years ago could have been part of a larger art theft ring, and now he could be working in this area. He could have framed John."

"But why?"

"Considering you don't know Red's real identity, it's hard to say. If you can figure out who he is, maybe you can find a connection with John. Or maybe John was just in the wrong place at the wrong time. What's your next move?"

"Trudy is going to ask around to see if she can get any more information from the owners of the galleries that were robbed. She's well connected, so if anyone can do it, she can. I guess we just need to wait. She seemed concerned that the thief will strike again, so I think she'll get right on it."

"That sounds like a solid plan."

"That's not all we learned. Trudy said that not only was Lena jealous of Darren's success, but that she was temperamental. She needs to stay on our list. She also confirmed what Maya said about Lena trying her hand at driftwood art."

"That means she would have had the tools to fashion the weapon," Anna said.

"My thoughts exactly. We should talk to Lena next. How about we visit the coffee shop where she works tomorrow and try to talk to her? I'm thinking that we'll have a better chance if we go after the breakfast rush. How about I pick you up at 10:00?"

After confirming their plans both for the next day and for dinner at Sydney's the following evening, they finished their meals, and each brought an herbal tea to the sunroom, where they continued chatting. Then Cassie went home early so Anna could get a good night's sleep after her long afternoon on the bike trail.

CHAPTER 9

On Wednesday morning, Cassie woke up to a text from Sydney, who was excited to be planning the menu for her first dinner guests in her new home. She planned to serve penne pasta with a vodka cream sauce and shrimp, which was her best entertaining dish. She wanted to run it by Cassie to make sure Anna didn't have any food allergies before she bought the ingredients. Cassie assured her that she did not and that they would bring dessert.

After a quick shower, she took Artie for a walk, then brought him to the inn. Cassie spent an hour in the gift shop, taking advantage of the slower morning to get to know Tyler, one of her new hires, and to make sure he felt supported.

She left Artie with Leslie and Tyler, and she and Anna headed to *Bobbi's Brews,* the coffee shop where Lena worked, for breakfast.

"I can't believe that tonight is your last night at the inn," Cassie said as they brought their coffee and breakfast sandwiches to a table. They recognized the thin young woman with straight auburn hair from the picture on her website.

Cassie had done some online research so they would know who they were looking for. She was busy with a customer, so they would have to wait a few minutes before trying to engage her in a conversation about Darren.

"I know. The change of scenery has really helped me to relax and get my mind off everything."

Anna closed her eyes for a moment.

"Is everything alright back at Seagull Cove?"

Anna's gaze became distant, then she pulled her attention back to Cassie and forced a smile. "Yes, of course. Everything's great. I'm really looking forward to our dinner with Sydney tonight. It's always nice to make a new friend."

Cassie wasn't convinced that everything was great, but she didn't want to make her friend feel uncomfortable, so she went with the subject change. "She's been a true friend, and I can already tell you two will get along famously. She's making a pasta dish that sounds amazing."

"Yum. I can't wait."

When they finished their breakfast sandwiches, there was a lull in foot traffic. Lena started to wipe down some nearby tables, so Cassie and Anna decided to make their move. As soon as she was within earshot, they struck up a conversation.

"It looks like we have another beautiful day before us," Anna said. "Since I'm only in town for a few days, I'm glad the weather is cooperating."

Lena turned and smiled. "May can be hit-or-miss in terms of the weather on Cape Cod. Sometimes it stays cool even into June, and other times, summer seems to start in May. New England weather always keeps things interesting."

"I'm an artist, so I'm looking forward to painting all the Cape Cod seasons," Cassie said.

Lena's large brown eyes sparkled. "I'm an artist, too. Sculpting is my passion. This job is only temporary." She pulled her phone from her pocket and showed them some photos of her work. "I've sold some of my pieces, but not enough to quit my day job." She glanced back to make sure her boss hadn't overheard her. "I shouldn't say that so loudly. I need this job."

"Your sculptures are beautiful," Cassie said. "Speaking of sculpting, did you hear about the driftwood artist who was murdered?"

"Darren Germain. He was a controversial character in the artist community. Of course, I always respected him and his work, but many others didn't." Cassie distinctly remembered that Trudy had said otherwise. And so did Maya, for that matter, although she wasn't as reliable a source as Trudy.

"I happened to admire his work, too," Anna said. "In fact, I had been wanting to purchase a cute little seahorse from him, but didn't get the chance."

"I haven't lived here long, but I've heard that many people —both in the artist community and the business world—were jealous of his rapid success," Cassie said.

"Well, there's only so much summer money to go around and when someone breezes into town and instantly becomes popular, it takes business away from others."

"But isn't that what free enterprise is all about?" Anna asked.

Lena let out a frustrated sigh. "Of course. But you know how people can be. And it wasn't just that. He collected his driftwood by trampling on sand dunes, so there's that, too."

"You're right," Cassie said. "No matter how beautiful his work was, he had no right to do that."

"His art was lovely. As a matter of fact, I was thinking of trying my hand at driftwood art. Maya Deveau, a local environmentalist, has been encouraging me to give it a try. She thought my sculpting skills would transfer nicely. In fact, she even brought me some wood that she collected to get started. She knows I would source my wood ethically, without walking on the dunes, since I'm on the board of her environmental committee."

"You should try it," Anna said.

"You seem like a fixture in the local art community," Cassie said. "Do you think another artist killed him? I am a new artist in town, just like Darren was, and I hate to think I'd receive such an unfriendly welcome."

"Oh, I wouldn't worry about that. Darren just rubbed people the wrong way."

Cassie hoped Lena was correct. When she first asked that question, she was trying to get the young woman to talk. But as the question left her mouth, she realized it was a legitimate fear. Perhaps the reason she sympathized with Darren so much was that she shared a few things in common with him that she hadn't consciously realized before.

Anna squeezed Cassie's forearm, apparently picking up on her discomfort.

"Besides," Lena said, "the killer may not be from Sand Dune Shores. He had a visitor staying with him at the time. They were in here for breakfast the morning Darren was killed, and I heard them in a heated argument. Maybe he's the one who killed Darren."

"Do you know his name?" Cassie asked.

"I think it was Jack. Or maybe Mac. I heard he checked into the *Sand Dune Inn* the night of Darren's murder."

A few customers walked into the coffee shop, so Lena excused herself and hopped behind the counter.

"That's interesting," Anna said.

"I'll say. We had another suspect right under our noses this whole time and we didn't know it."

"I completely forgot until Lena just mentioned it, but when we saw him on the beach, Darren told us he had a houseguest. He made some sort of sarcastic comment about everyone wanting a piece of you when you're successful."

"Are you thinking what I'm thinking?" Cassie asked.

Anna nodded. "We should get back to the inn to see if he's still there."

Cassie glanced at the clock behind the counter. "Checkout is at 11:00. We should leave now, just in case he was planning to check out today."

They drove back to the inn, and Cassie brought Anna to the office, which was located between the restaurant and the Hardings' private residence, so that she could access the computer and see if he had a checkout date.

"She said his first name was either Jack or Mac," Anna said.

Cassie opened the registration software and scanned the current guests. "Bingo. There is only one single male who checked in on Monday night. Mac Dalton. He's in my old room, upstairs. He reserved it until Friday morning."

"Let's knock on the door and see if he's there. We can always tell him that we wanted to extend our condolences because we are the ones who discovered the body," Anna said.

"Great idea. Let's go."

CHAPTER 10

The women climbed the staircase and proceeded to the end of the corridor, where Mac Dalton's room was located. Cassie knocked on the door to the room that she had happily called home while she waited for her memory to return.

It was funny how time obscured memories. Now, she thought fondly of her time at the inn, but while she was living it, all she could think about was getting her memory back.

A man in his late fifties with disheveled greying hair and a hunter green t-shirt that was half tucked into his faded blue jeans opened the door.

He looked at Cassie. "I'm all set. I don't need anything."

"I'm sorry?" Cassie said.

"Don't you work for the inn? I thought I saw you working behind the counter in the gift shop."

"Of course. Yes, I do, but that's not why I came by."

He gave her a confused look.

"I'm Cassie, and this is my friend, Anna. We understand that you were friends with Darren Germain."

He nodded.

"We are the ones who found his body. We came to offer you our condolences," Cassie said.

"Would it be okay if we came in for a minute?" Anna asked.

"I'm not really in the mood to talk and there's not much space in here, so...."

"We'll make it quick," Cassie said as they quickly stepped inside. Empty beer bottles and an empty pizza box littered the windowsill. The table and chairs where Cassie painted while she lived there were hidden beneath a pile of clothes. It looked like the same room, but it didn't feel like it at all. The clutter was making her anxious. She would have turned around and left, but they needed to speak with Mac.

"Sorry for the mess. I didn't feel like being with people the last couple of nights, so I ate up here and had a few beers in honor of Darren." He scooped up the clothes from the chairs and dumped them onto the bed. Then he walked over to the mini fridge and grabbed a bottle of beer. "Can I offer you ladies a cold one?"

They both shook their heads, so he opened his bottle and sat amidst the pile of clothes on the bed.

Cassie and Anna sat at the table.

"We're so sorry for your loss," Cassie said.

"We saw Darren on the beach Monday afternoon, and he offered me a coupon for one of his pieces of driftwood art," Anna added. "That's why we were at his studio and how we ended up discovering his body."

He took a long swig of beer. Cassie couldn't help but wonder if he was trying to drink away his grief or his guilt.

"Do you have any idea who might have done this to Darren?" Anna asked.

He pulled his feet onto the bed and sat cross-legged. "None at all. He had his quirks, but I've never known him to have an enemy who wanted to see him dead. I wish he'd never moved to this town."

"Why did he move here?" Anna asked. "We heard he was a newcomer."

"He had been living on the coast of New Hampshire, making driftwood carvings. He thought the Cape would offer a better market for them, with what he used to call 'upscale tourists.'"

"Is there anyone from his past that could have resurfaced and killed him? It seems like the police are focusing on local artists, environmentalists, and business owners. Do you think he could have had an enemy from his past?"

"Not that I can think of. But that doesn't mean there wasn't."

"How long had you been staying with him before he died?" Cassie asked. "Did he give you any indication that he felt he was in danger?"

"I had just arrived. I was visiting a friend in Boston over the weekend, and I came to Sand Dune Shores early on Monday. We had breakfast together, then he wanted to collect some driftwood. We were supposed to meet back at his house later that day, but when I went back there, it was, well, a crime scene. That's when I checked in here. In the short amount of time that I spent with him, he didn't seem worried about anything, and he certainly didn't say anything about being afraid for his life. I think whatever happened took him by surprise." Darren paused, his gaze fixed on Cassie as if searching his memory. "I overheard a conversation in the dining room about a staff member at the inn who recently helped the police solve some crimes. Is that you?"

"Anna and I both have experience helping the police," Cassie said.

He took a notepad and pen from the nightstand drawer and jotted something down. "In that case, here's my cell phone number. Please let me know if you learn anything about his death. I wish I could be more helpful."

"We mainly came to express our condolences." Cassie didn't want to reveal how much they were actually investigating, in case Mac was dangerous. She had the sense he wasn't being completely honest."But since we're discussing Darren's murder, you might be able to shed light on something. We talked to someone who believes that Darren's business could have been a front for something illegal. Do you think that's possible?"

Mac chuckled and shook his head. "Darren was quirky, but I've never known him to do anything illegal. I think they're mistaken."

"There's something else we need to ask you. You were overheard arguing with Darren at breakfast on Monday. What was that about?"

Cassie braced herself for a hostile response, but Mac just chuckled again. "If I had a dollar for every disagreement Darren and I had, I'd be a rich man. Let me think… that one was about whether the Red Sox would go all the way this year. I don't mean to be rude, but I'd rather be alone right now."

"Of course," Cassie said. "I just have one more question. When we were in his studio, we noticed some pieces of driftwood that were painted with inspirational quotes. Things like,

'From above, all is clear.' And 'Nature speaks to those who listen.'"

"I think another one said, 'Sand shifts, but truth remains,'" Anna added.

"They almost sound religious. Was he a religious man?" Cassie asked.

"Maybe a little philosophical, but I wouldn't say religious. My guess would be that someone commissioned them."

"That's what we thought, too," Cassie said. "We won't take up any more of your time."

"You should try to get out of this room," Anna said. "It might do you some good."

"Maybe I'll get dinner at the bar in the tavern tonight. I was going to leave town after Darren passed, but I want to stick around to see if the police come up with any answers."

"Who is going to take care of his estate?" Cassie asked.

"His only family was his brother, Scott. They weren't close, but I'd imagine he'll take care of it."

They thanked Mac for his time and left.

"Did you believe Mac?" Cassie asked after she was sure they were out of earshot.

"There's something about him that seemed off, but I can't place my finger on it."

"Same here," Cassie said. "I felt like he was hiding something. I don't think we can rule him out."

"Me, either. But there is one thing I do know. We need a break from all this sleuthing," Cassie said. "I told Sydney we'd bring dessert tonight. Let's go pick something up. The local grocery store has a good bakery. Then we can sit on my porch and enjoy the afternoon sun."

"Sounds good to me," Anna said.

The women went to the grocery store and decided to get some vanilla cake mix and chocolate frosting so they could bake the dessert themselves. On the way home, they stopped for a bottle of wine, then spun back by the inn to pick up Artie.

They took him for a walk on the beach. The sound of the waves crashing on the hard sand relaxed Cassie. She inhaled deeply. Although there was still a lot of work to do on behalf of John Seewald, she was optimistic about the future. She had new friends, a new home, and she lived within driving distance of her father and brother.

They walked at a leisurely pace. As they passed by the dune, they couldn't help but stop. They walked to its base and watched the movement of the sea grass as the wind blew through it. They turned to continue walking when a piece of weathered wood caught Cassie's eye. She picked it up and discovered that it had another saying painted on it. This one said, 'A message for those who rise above.'

"That's a strange quote," Anna said. "It shares the same philosophical theme as the others, but it's so vague."

"I should take it to Rick in case it's important," Cassie said.

When they got back to the beach house, the women mixed the ingredients for the cake and put it in the oven. Then they sat on the porch with a glass of iced tea and let the sun warm their faces.

When the oven timer went off, Cassie took it out to let it cool before frosting it, refilled their glasses, and they continued lounging on the deck.

At 4:00, they frosted the cake and put it in a cake dish. Then Cassie went next door to get a painting she had made for Sydney as a housewarming gift.

Anna admired the painting of the yellow Cape Cod style home with a white picket fence. "That is lovely," Anna said. "Is that her new house?"

Cassie nodded. "I was with Sydney when she saw it for the first time. It was love at first sight."

"I can see why. It's picture-perfect. She's going to love this painting."

Cassie wrapped the painting in brown paper, then they carefully loaded the painting, the cake, and the wine into Cassie's SUV, and headed out.

CHAPTER 11

On their way to Sydney's, they stopped at the police station to give Rick the piece of driftwood they had found by the sand dune. They tried to fish for information on the case but were unsuccessful, so they left without learning anything new.

Just before 5:00, Cassie pulled into Sydney's driveway.

Anna brought the cake and wine while Cassie carefully carried the wrapped painting into the house. Before they could ring the doorbell, the white door swung open. Sydney was about to blurt something out, but she stopped when she saw the painting.

"It's a housewarming gift for you." Cassie took it into the entryway, where Sydney unwrapped it.

She stepped back to admire it. "It's beautiful, Cassie. Thank you so much." She carried it into the living room. "I know the perfect spot."

Anna brought the cake and wine and placed it on the dining room table. Then Sydney showed them a wall next to the bay window in the living room where she intended to put the painting. As she held it up, she asked, "What do you think?"

"It's perfect," Cassie said.

"I agree. I'll hang it later. Let's eat while dinner is hot."

"It smells amazing in here," Anna said.

Sydney looped her arm through Anna's. "Thanks so much for coming."

They took the long way to the dining room so Sydney could give Anna a tour of the downstairs, including the first-floor bedroom, which she had set up as an office. They passed through the bright kitchen to the dining room, where the table was set with a baby blue tablecloth with yellow accents.

"Fancy," Cassie said.

"I figured I'd go all out for my first dinner party," she said, smiling proudly.

They showed Sydney the cake they had made, which said 'Congratulations Sydney.' Cassie chuckled as she pointed to the small picture on the cake. "I tried to draw a house with decorator gel, but apparently I do better with paintbrushes."

Anna laughed. "I guess it's not a transferrable skill, but it will still taste good."

Sydney brought the cake to the counter and opened the bottle of Riesling.

Cassie and Anna helped her bring the salad and the penne pasta with vodka cream sauce and shrimp to the table, and they all sat down.

"You've outdone yourself, Sydney," Cassie said. "I knew you were a good cook, but I had no idea you could make a dish like this."

"I love to cook when I have the time, but I haven't had the space to entertain. Now that I have this house, I'm going to make it a priority. I can't wait to have my family over, and the Hardings, too."

While they ate, Anna had lots of questions about Sydney's career writing children's books, and Anna told Sydney more about her move to Seagull Cove and her ice cream shop.

"My sister and I shared a counseling practice in Boston, and she always had this fantasy of opening an ice cream parlor that would become a community hub. We frequented an ice cream shop down the street from our practice, and she once remarked that the little shop, with all it did to foster a sense of community in the neighborhood, did more for people's mental health than counseling did."

"I doubt that," Cassie said.

"I didn't get the impression she was downplaying the importance of our work. Many problems are more complicated than what a fun evening with ice cream and friends can fix. But I understood what she meant. In our busy culture, we need more ways to gather and connect with others. About five years after she died in a boating accident, I needed a change, so I moved to Seagull Cove, where we often vacationed, and opened a shop called *Bella's Dream*. It's been a year, and I haven't regretted my decision. I've made some great friends, who have become like family. Cassie had the chance to meet some of them when she stayed in town after her car accident."

"If I'm ever in Seagull Cove, I'll be sure to come by," Sydney said.

"Please do. I'd love to show you around."

When they finished eating, they brought their plates to the kitchen. Cassie and Sydney rinsed them and loaded the dishwasher while Anna sliced the cake and brought three generous slices to the table.

"It seemed like you were about to tell us something when we first arrived," Anna said after a couple of bites of cake. "It looked like you were about to say something, but then you stopped when you saw Cassie's housewarming gift."

"Oh, my goodness, you're right. I completely forgot when I saw the painting!"

"What was it?" Cassie asked.

"My mother came by yesterday, and it turns out that Maya was at Darren's studio the afternoon he was killed."

"Are you sure?" Cassie asked.

"Yes. My mother knew how much I loved Darren's work, so she went to his studio to choose a piece for my new home. She chose a beautiful lighthouse, which I put in my office. My mom didn't think that Maya saw her, because she was arriving as my mom was leaving. They only passed each other in their cars, but my mother recognized her, because she and my mom chatted on the beach one afternoon when I lived at your beach house."

"Did she tell Rick about it?"

"She told him as soon as she learned of Darren's death."

"I wish we had a way to get into Darren's studio to look around again. After we found his body, we only had a couple of minutes before the police arrived. I can't help but think that we might be able to find another clue if we had more time to look around," Cassie said, glancing at Anna.

"I know what you're thinking," Sydney said. "But how would we get in? Besides, we could get into a lot of trouble. Isn't it still a crime scene?"

"Not necessarily," Cassie said. "The police are probably finished with it by now."

"But still, I don't want to ruin your first dinner party. Maybe Anna and I could go tomorrow."

"And have Anna spend her last day in Sand Dune Shores sneaking around a murder scene? No. If you're going to do it, tonight would be the time."

"It *would* be better to go at night," Sydney agreed. "I'll consider this an exciting turn of events. Not many people can say their first dinner party ends in sleuthing."

"More like breaking and entering," Anna said. "But we won't think about that."

The women put their dessert dishes in the sink, then Sydney drove them to Darren's showroom.

"What exactly are we looking for?" Sydney asked.

"I'm not sure. Anything that might give us some insight into what happened on Monday," Cassie said.

"Try to imagine yourself as the killer," Anna said.

"If it was Maya, she probably got the murder weapon from Darren's shop. I suppose she could have made it before she came, but she wouldn't have easy access to the proper tools like Lena would."

The women exited the car and quietly closed the door. As they made their way toward the building, a light went on in the back.

"That's the light to his workspace, not the showroom," Cassie said. "But who could that be? There's no other car here."

"The lights could have an automatic sensor. Maybe there's nobody there," Sydney suggested.

"I don't think we're close enough to set off a sensor," Anna said. "I think there's someone back there."

"A critter?" Sydney asked.

"Let's go and see," Cassie said. "There could be a car parked in the back."

The women walked closer.

"We should just call the police," Sydney said. "This feels dangerous."

"But then we'd have to explain why we are here after hours," Cassie pointed out.

"I agree," Anna said. "Let's sneak around back and see who it is. We'll hide so they don't see us."

Sydney gripped her car key. "Okay. I'll keep my key out so we can run back to my car and make a quick getaway if we need to."

They crept around to the side of the building and stopped suddenly when they saw a black SUV with the trunk opened.

"You guys stay here," Cassie whispered. "That way, if he or she is dangerous, you'll be able to run and call for help."

Despite her friends' protests, Cassie slipped closer to the car. Her eyes focused on a trunk filled with driftwood art. The next thing she knew, there was a flashlight shining in her eyes.

"Mac, is that you?" she asked, squinting to protect her eyes. "What on earth are you doing?"

CHAPTER 12

Mac's shoulders sank when he saw Cassie standing there. Once she ascertained that he didn't have a weapon, she called over Anna and Sydney.

"You have a lot of explaining to do," Sydney said when she saw the trunk. "You're stealing artwork from your supposed friend."

"I'm not stealing anything. It's not what it looks like," Mac protested.

Cassie looked at the art in the trunk, then back at Mac. "You're not sneaking into Darren's showroom after dark and taking his driftwood art? Because that's exactly what it looks like."

"Well, yes. That part is true. But I have a legitimate reason for doing this."

Cassie pulled her phone from her pocket. "Unless your reason involves the police giving you permission to be here—which I doubt since you're creeping around at night—then I don't care what your reason is. I'm calling Detective Blaney."

"Wait! Please don't. Give me a chance to explain."

Cassie looked at Anna, who shrugged her shoulders. "It can't hurt to hear him out."

"Alright. I'll give you five minutes to explain. Make them count."

"And keep your hands where we can see them," Anna added.

"It's true that Darren and I were old friends. But we had a falling out shortly before he left New Hampshire and moved to Sand Dune Shores."

"That sounds like it could be a motive for murder," Cassie said.

"It's not like that. A few years ago, Darren borrowed some money from me, but he couldn't pay me back. That's why he moved to Sand Dune Shores. He thought there would be a bigger market on Cape Cod for his driftwood art, and it turned out he was right. He became more successful than even he imagined he would. A couple of months ago, after he got back on his feet, he called me and asked me to come for a visit. He said he finally had the money to pay me back. But before he had a chance to do that, he was murdered."

"So, you decided to steal his art?" Cassie asked.

He let out a sigh. "I guess I didn't think it through all the way. But I was only taking back what was mine. I figured I could sell these pieces back in New Hampshire and recoup some of my loss. I figured they might fetch an even higher price now that he's gone."

Cassie shook her head. "You're profiting off his death."

"Now, don't go judging me," Mac said. "I would never do anything like this if he didn't owe me a lot of money." He glanced into the trunk. "This won't even cover the loan, but at least it won't be a total loss."

"You mean it wouldn't have been," Sydney said. "You can't possibly think that we won't call the police. How do we even know that you are telling the truth?"

Mac ran his hand through his thick hair. "Fine. I'll put everything back where I found it. But don't call the police."

Cassie looked at Anna. "We'd have a hard time explaining to Rick why we are here at night, too. Technically speaking, we're also trespassing."

A glimmer of hope crossed his face.

"I don't know," Anna said. "Rick is reasonable, and he knows you have a history of getting involved in investigations. He'd probably reprimand you, but I don't think anyone would press charges. On the other hand, withholding this information from the police could get us all into trouble."

Mac's eyes darted between the women. "What if I can prove that I'm not the killer? Would you consider forgetting about what happened here tonight? You can watch me put everything back."

"How are you going to prove that?" Cassie asked.

"Just give me twenty-four hours. We'll meet in the library at the inn tomorrow evening at 7:00, and I guarantee you that I'll have the evidence to prove my innocence."

"How do we know we can trust you?" Cassie asked. Although secretly she thought his offer was more intriguing than she let on.

"What do you have to lose? If I can't provide the evidence, then you can go to the police."

"He does sound confident," Anna said.

"That's because I am. Why would I kill someone who owed me money?"

"Either because you're lying about that, or Darren refused to pay you back, so you killed him in a moment of rage."

"Even if that were true, wouldn't I have taken the art the night I supposedly killed him? The police told me that his body was discovered at least an hour after he died. I would have had plenty of time to take the art and leave town."

The women looked at each other.

"He does bring up a good point," Anna said.

"Alright," Cassie said. "We'll meet you tomorrow night at 7:00 in the library. But if you don't show up, we're going straight to the police."

Mac breathed a sigh of relief. "Fair enough. I'll unload the trunk."

The women watched as Mac returned the art to the showroom and tucked the spare key underneath the mat by the entrance to Darren's private residence. Then he got into his truck and drove away.

"Should we still take a look around while we're here?" Cassie asked.

"We might as well," Anna said. "We've come this far."

"You two don't give up, do you?" Sydney said. "My nerves are shot. Why don't I wait in the car? I'll keep watch to make sure nobody is coming."

"Good idea," Cassie said.

Cassie and Anna went upstairs, and Cassie took the key from under the mat where Mac had left it.

"Let's look around his apartment first," Cassie said.

They scanned the small apartment, but at first glance, there was nothing out of the ordinary.

Anna went to his bedroom while Cassie looked through the drawers in the tiny kitchen.

"Anything?" Anna asked when she returned from the bedroom.

Cassie shook her head.

"Nothing here, either. We might as well take a closer look around his studio since we've already…"

"Broken and entered?" Cassie asked.

"I was going to say, 'come this far,' but that works, too."

The women descended the outdoor staircase and entered the showroom.

"Everything looks just how it did on Monday," Anna said, after closely examining the space.

"Let's look in his workspace again."

They walked toward the back and took a look around.

"What's in that notebook?" Cassie asked.

"I don't know. Was that here on Monday?"

"It could have been." Cassie picked it up and opened it. "It's a sketchpad."

Anna looked over her shoulders as she flipped through the pages. "What are those drawings?"

"I have no idea. It looks like some sort of configuration of driftwood, but I can't tell what it's supposed to be." Cassie snapped a photo of the sketches. Then she studied them again. "Whatever the project is, it requires a lot of driftwood. Maybe someone commissioned something for their garden."

"It could be," Anna said.

"I don't think we'll find anything else here. We should go."

"I'll bring the key back to the mat," Anna said, locking the door to the showroom.

When Anna returned, they got back into the car. "Let's stop by the inn to make sure Mac's car is in the parking lot," Cassie suggested.

When they arrived at the inn, his car was there.

"Let's walk Anna inside," Cassie said to Sydney. "Then I'll come back to your house to get my car."

"Alright. I want to see the picture of the sketchpad, anyway," Sydney said.

The women went to the library where they wouldn't be overheard and showed Sydney the sketches. She agreed that they were probably for some type of garden art.

"Do you think we made a mistake in trusting Mac?" Anna asked.

"I think it was the right decision, although I'm not convinced that Mac is innocent. He could have killed Darren in a moment of rage and only thought of stealing the artwork later. That could be why he went back tonight," Cassie said.

"We can make a final decision about whether to trust him tomorrow evening, when we see what his so-called evidence is. I don't think he'd go back to Darren's tonight and take the art. He knows we'd go to the police, and if he skipped town, they would easily be able to find him," Anna said.

"I agree," Cassie said. "That would be pretty dumb."

"It certainly has been an exciting last night for you in Sand Dune Shores," Sydney said.

Anna grinned. "There never seems to be a dull moment when Cassie and I are together. I'm looking forward to talking with Mac tomorrow evening."

"It sounds like you're planning to stay in town until our meeting with Mac is over. After that, we'll keep you posted on everything so you can help us solve the case long distance."

"Or…" Anna said.

Cassie's eyes flew open. Was Anna about to say what she hoped she was?

"Or I could stay on a few more days. I hate to leave when things are starting to get exciting."

"I would *love* that," Cassie said. "But this weekend is Memorial Day. Aren't you needed at your ice cream shop?"

"Let me call Velma and see how she feels about my staying. She's taking care of things while I'm away. I don't think she'd mind if I stayed until Saturday. She's always telling me I should take more time off, anyway." Anna tapped on her cell phone and stepped out of the library. She returned five minutes later. "Velma has no problem covering for me through the weekend. How about if I stay until Saturday? Even if we can't solve the case by then, at least we'll make some more progress."

"Yay," Cassie said.

"Awesome," Sydney added. "With the two of you working together, I'm sure you'll solve it faster."

"You should move your things to my house tomorrow, since the inn is full for the weekend," Cassie said.

"That might work out better. Being under the same roof will help us stay more focused."

"It's settled then," Cassie said.

Elizabeth popped her head into the library. "I thought I heard voices coming from here. What's all the excitement about?"

"Anna's going to remain in town for a few more days. She's going to stay at my house."

"Wonderful," Elizabeth said. "The weather is supposed to be beautiful for the next few days." She turned to leave, but stopped suddenly. "Wait. Does this have something to do with solving Darren's murder?"

"Maybe just a tiny bit," Cassie said, holding her thumb and

index finger slightly apart. "What do you think of Mac Dalton? Was there anything strange about his behavior when he checked in on Monday?"

Elizabeth narrowed her brow. "I mean, his friend had just gotten murdered, so he seemed a bit preoccupied. But nothing unusual for having just received tragic news. Why? Do you suspect him of murdering Darren?"

Cassie didn't want to cause Elizabeth any unnecessary anxiety. "You know me. I like to consider everything."

"You ladies be careful," she said as she was leaving. "I know from experience how dangerous things can get."

"Elizabeth is right," Cassie said. "Even if Mac was acting strangely, it may not mean he was guilty. He did just find out that his friend was murdered."

"It's been a long evening," Anna said. "Let's go back to Sydney's and help her clean up."

"Don't worry about that. It's just a few dessert dishes. I'll have it done in no time."

"In that case, I'll come back with you to get my car. Anna, shall we meet up for breakfast?"

"Absolutely. I'll see you tomorrow morning."

CHAPTER 13

On Thursday morning, Cassie took Artie for a walk along the beach before giving him an overdue bath and bringing him to the gift shop. Leslie was training a new hire, Eli. As a retired teacher, she excelled at mentoring new employees and seemed to enjoy it, so Cassie scheduled new staff to work with her whenever possible. With everyone getting up to speed, the shop seemed well prepared for the upcoming tourist season.

Just as Cassie was leaving the gift shop to meet Anna in the dining room, Jake popped in.

"What brings you to the inn so early?" Cassie asked.

"I wanted to touch base about…" He glanced over his shoulder to see if the staff was within earshot.

"I was just about to grab a table for breakfast. Why don't we talk there?"

Jake joined Cassie at her usual out-of-the-way corner table. "I was thinking about our conversation with Trudy. If this Red guy really did frame John, and if he's the one behind the robberies in this area, it seems likely that he must have some sort of warehouse where he's storing the stolen art," Jake said.

"That makes sense. I doubt he'd store it at his house, where it could easily be traced to him, and he'd need to hold on to it for a while before selling it."

"Exactly. Since I knew you were busy with Anna and with Darren's case, I did some research. I figured wherever he stored the art would need to be both climatized and hidden."

"Like a storage unit under a fake name," Cassie said. "But there must be tons of those in the area. Besides, it's not like we could visit each one and ask if any of their clients have red hair. They wouldn't give us that information, even if they knew it."

"That's true. But I called Trudy and asked for a list of galleries that had been broken into over the past six months, and there are three. They all happened within weeks of each other. I also paid Rick a visit to see if he knew anything. Only one of the galleries falls within his jurisdiction, but he is aware of the other two, and he believes it's the same thief. He also said that so far, there haven't been any robberies at any other galleries on the Cape in the past six months. He's been checking regularly."

"That's interesting," Cassie said. "John must have known that. It could be how he knew that Red was in this area."

"He never told you why he suspected that?" Jake asked.

Cassie shook her head. "Unfortunately, he never did. He believed that the less I knew, the safer I was. He never even mentioned whether he knew the identity of the man who supposedly framed him, or that he went by Red. He made it clear that I was only there for moral support and for my knowledge of art. He thought I could get better information from the gallery owners. John said that this guy was dangerous, but he felt he had nothing left to lose. So, he was trying to tell me as little as possible."

"It's ironic that he is the one who ended up getting killed, and you are now investigating alone," Jake said. "But I appreciate him wanting to keep you safe. Anyway, I narrowed it down to ten potential storage facilities, but as you said, there's no point in visiting them. And without Red's real name, it wouldn't matter, even if we could convince them to give us the information. Try to think, Cassie. Do you have any idea what John's plan was during your time in Sand Dune Shores?"

"I know that he had meetings scheduled with some gallery owners, so I assume they were the ones whose galleries were broken into—likely the three on your list."

"And Trudy is looking into those for us," Jake said.

"There was one more meeting that he mentioned, but I don't remember the details."

"Try to think, Cassie."

She searched her mind. It felt like a lifetime ago. "I know that he had a meeting planned for our first day in town. I think the guy's name was Leo. He told me to dress warmly because it would be freezing."

"It was February at the time," Jake said. "That could be anywhere."

"Wait a minute!" Cassie said. "He said to bring my raincoat because we would be by the water, and it would be windy. It could have been at a marina or some docks."

"There are some loading docks near the *Sand Dune Shores Marina,* with a warehouse on the premises. Maybe it was there."

A wave of optimism swept over Cassie. "It could have been. It's worth a try."

Jake checked his watch. "I have to get back to work now, but how about we go first thing tomorrow morning? Those guys start work early, so morning might be the best time to catch them, anyway."

"That sounds like a plan."

"What sounds like a plan?"

Cassie looked up to find Anna standing there.

"I'll let you explain," Jake said to Cassie. "I've gotta run."

Cassie relayed their conversation to Anna. "I'm glad Jake and I are not going to the docks until tomorrow. That will give us today to focus on Darren's case. Who is your top suspect?"

"I'm not sure yet. According to Sydney's mom, Maya lied to us about being at Darren's showroom the day he died," Anna said.

"That could either mean she's guilty, or she is innocent, but decided to withhold that information because it would make her *look* guilty."

"The tricky part will be figuring out which it is," Anna said. "And I still don't trust Mac. I'm curious about what so-called evidence he will bring tonight to prove his innocence."

"And then there's Lena," Cassie said.

"Not to mention Chet Mercer. But I think he has the weakest motive. I know he was protective of local businesses, but I don't see him killing for that."

"Me, either. But we shouldn't rule him out. People have killed for lesser things," Cassie said.

"True. Chet also thought that Darren's art business might have been a cover for something shady, such as money laundering, but I think he was wrong about that. From what we learned, Darren's showroom was always busy, and he collected a lot of driftwood to make his many pieces," Anna said.

"And his art did command a hefty price, as we saw from the price tags when we were at his showroom," Cassie added.

"Agreed. I think it's safe to say that his newfound wealth came from his art. I think we can rule out Chet's theory."

"However, I don't think it's a coincidence that Darren was murdered with a driftwood stake. Someone was trying to send a message. Either they disapproved of his artwork or the way he collected wood," Cassie said.

"If that's the case, it could be Maya. She had strong feelings about his wood-collecting practices. Or for that matter, it could have been Lena, who was jealous of his success."

"In terms of our next move, now that we know Maya was lying to us, I think we should talk to her again," Cassie said.

"Agreed. Let's take another walk over there after breakfast."

CHAPTER 14

The women enjoyed a leisurely breakfast before walking to Maya's house.

"I think I see Maya on her deck," Cassie said as they turned the corner.

"I do, too. Let's go around to the back."

When she spotted the women, Maya ducked into the house.

"That didn't feel like a coincidence," Cassie said.

"You're right. I get the feeling she's avoiding us. Let's ring the doorbell."

Cassie rang the doorbell, but nobody answered.

"Maybe she went back out to the deck," Anna said, darting back around the house. "Nope, she's inside," she reported when she returned. "She's definitely avoiding us."

"Sounds like a guilty conscience to me." Cassie rang the doorbell again.

"We can't force her to come to the door," Anna said. "It's not a crime to refuse to talk to us."

"Let's try one more time. Maya, it's Cassie and Anna,"

Cassie shouted in as friendly a voice as she could muster. "We just have a few questions about Monday afternoon, and we'd rather not go to the police with the information we have. We're guessing there's an explanation, and we'd rather hear it from you."

Cassie heard footsteps.

"I think she's coming," Anna said.

The door slowly opened, revealing a reluctant Maya on the other side.

"Can we talk for a few minutes?" Cassie asked.

Maya stepped back so they could enter, and the women sat in the living room. "I think I know why you're here. I saw the two of you at the inn with Sydney last night while I was eating at the bar. I'm guessing she told you that her mother saw me driving to Darren's showroom as she was leaving."

Cassie nodded.

"I swear that when I left, he was alive and well," Maya said. "I went to try to reason with him about the sand dunes. After Darren left the beach on Monday, I snapped a photo of the portion of the sand dune where he had walked. I showed him that it was starting to erode, and I begged him to stay off it. I told him I was going to the police with my pictures, and he said that it was worth it to him to pay the fine to do what he needed to do. I'll admit that I was angry, but I didn't kill him. I had a different plan. I was building a case against him to have him banned from our beach." She pulled out her phone and swiped through several photos of Darren climbing the dune. They were clearly taken on different days, because he was wearing different clothing. Ironically, in most of the photos, he was marching right by the sign that warned patrons to stay off the dune.

"How do we know you didn't lose your temper when he refused to stay off the dune?" Cassie asked.

"Because I had asked Rick a few months before what it would take to get him permanently banned, and he said that if I could prove that he was ignoring the warnings, he'd see what he could do about it. Why would I kill him when I had a plan to get him banned? I'm telling you, the killer must have been someone whose livelihood was threatened by Darren's presence in town."

"You mean someone like Lena?" Anna asked.

"Yes, like Lena. Or someone else who would rather he not be around," Maya said. "I figured it was only a matter of time until the police realized that I was at Darren's place the afternoon he died. So, I've been asking around a bit myself. It turns out that Wade Townsend also might have had a motive to kill Darren."

"Who's Wade Townsend?" Cassie asked. "That name sounds familiar."

"You've probably seen him on TV. He owns a car dealership in town, and he makes those ridiculous commercials."

Cassie smiled. "I know who you mean. He's the guy who's always looking at the wrong camera, right?"

"That's the one. My sources tell me that his girlfriend, Cindy, had been spending a lot of time with Darren, and Wade wasn't happy about it. He thought Darren was trying to steal her away. They were even overheard arguing about it at a bar one night."

"So, you think Wade killed Darren because he wouldn't stay away from Cindy?"

"It's possible. Everyone knows that Wade has a temper, and he didn't like to be shown up."

"I know where his dealership is. We could take a ride over and ask him a few questions," Cassie said.

"You should do that. He's always there," Maya said.

"Just a piece of advice. You really should tell the police that you were at Darren's on Monday," Anna said. "It's going to look a lot worse for you if they find out on their own, and as you said, it's only a matter of time."

The women knew that Sydney's mom had already told Rick, but if she were innocent, she would still be better off telling them herself.

Maya sighed. "I suppose you're right."

Since they weren't going to get any more information from her, Cassie and Anna left.

"Do you believe Maya?" Cassie asked as they walked back to the inn to get her car.

"I couldn't get a clear read on her. She might be guilty, but I also understand why she wouldn't admit to being at Darren's, even if she were innocent. Still, she had a lot of anger toward him, so I can see her losing her temper."

"Me, too. Even if she did have a plan to get Darren banned from the beach."

"I agree," Cassie said. "Even if he were banned from your beach, he still could have done the same thing in other locations. I could see her taking matters into her own hands."

"How are we going to get Wade Townsend to talk to us?" Anna asked.

"I think I have an idea. Follow my lead when we get there."

They drove across town to Wade Townsend's Ford dealership and were greeted by a young man who stood immediately when they walked in. "Hi, ladies." He glanced out at

Cassie's SUV. "It looks like your car has a few miles on it. Don't worry. You've come to the right place."

Cassie scanned the dealership. "Is that Wade Townsend over there?" she asked.

"It is, but he's busy. I'd be more than happy to help you," the salesman said.

"My friend really has her heart set on speaking with Wade," Anna said. "She saw one of his commercials, and she wants to talk to him directly. I don't think you're going to persuade her to work with anyone else."

Seeing that he wasn't getting anywhere, the young man approached Wade Townsend, who came over wearing a charming smile. "Hello, ladies. I understand one of you is in the market for a car. What exactly are you looking for?"

"I'm thinking about a white Mustang convertible," Cassie said.

Anna looked at her wide-eyed. Cassie suppressed a smirk, realizing that Anna couldn't tell if she was serious or not. If Cassie was honest with herself, she wasn't sure, either.

"I'd like to test drive one, if possible."

"Of course," he said. "If you could give me your license, I'll need to make a copy of it. Then I'll grab the keys to a fully loaded Mustang that just came in. You're going to love it. It takes the corners like a dream."

Cassie handed over her license, and Wade left to make a photocopy.

Anna chuckled. "You're test driving this convertible for real, aren't you?"

"Kind of. But I'm not going to buy one today. I want to test drive a few other models first."

Cassie got into the driver's seat and Anna got in the back,

while Wade sat up front doing his best to sell the vehicle. It felt amazing to have the wind whipping through her hair as the sun shone on her back. She could definitely get used to this. "How does it handle in the winter?"

"This isn't your father's convertible. They've come a long way. They handle beautifully in the New England ice and snow."

Cassie pulled over.

"What are you doing?" Wade asked.

"I'd like to drive it with the top up as well, since I'll also be using it during the winter months." But her true reason was because it was too noisy to have a proper conversation with Wade while the roof was down.

"That's smart," Wade said. He pushed a button, and the roof appeared. Then he raised the latch handle to secure it.

Cassie pulled back onto the road and took the long way back to the dealership.

"I just recently moved to Sand Dune Shores," Cassie said. "I hope I made the right choice. Did you hear that there was a murder in town?"

"I did," Wade said. "What a tragedy. But Sand Dune Shores has always been a safe little town. Don't let that put you off. And it's the perfect place to drive a convertible. Can't you just imagine the salty air in your lungs while you're driving by the beach?"

Cassie nodded and smiled. She really could.

"Did you know the victim?" Anna asked, evidently trying to steer the conversation back to Darren.

Wade seemed torn between wanting to change the subject and wanting to keep the conversation going so he could sell a car.

"I'd seen him around, but I wouldn't say I knew him."

They were starting to get closer to the dealership.

"I hear he was quite the ladies' man," Cassie said.

Wade gave a slight eye roll. "Not as much as he thought he was. But I suppose some women are attracted to the tortured artist type. If you ask me, that artist persona was a phony one. The guy was making a killing on his art." He glanced at Cassie. "Sorry. Poor choice of words."

"I know the type," Cassie said. "Did a lot of women fall for that?"

"You'd be surprised," Wade said. He winked at her. "Not the bright ones though."

Cassie tried not to laugh at his not-so-veiled attempt to charm her.

"You know, the police even questioned me about his death," Wade said. "He would flirt with my girlfriend all the time and it would annoy me. I told him off more than once, and I guess someone overheard me. It's lucky for me that I was working at the dealership all day, or I'd probably be a suspect."

"I see," Cassie said. "Who do you think did it?"

He hesitated. "I think it was one of the local artists. I heard Lena Heins was pretty jealous of his success."

Cassie pulled into the parking lot of the dealership.

"What did you think?" Wade asked.

"It's a big decision. I'd like to test drive some other cars before committing, but it's a strong contender."

"Well, you just let me know what you decide, and I'll take good care of you."

CHAPTER 15

Cassie and Anna got back into Cassie's car and drove off the lot.

"I love that your test drive wasn't just a cover story," Anna said. "What did you really think of the car?"

"I was telling Wade the truth. I want to test drive some others, but I think it's safe to say that my next car will be a convertible."

"Well, at least it wasn't a total loss. Wade has an alibi, but you got to test drive one of the convertibles on your list."

"It's definitely a contender. My first car was a pre-owned baby blue Mustang back in the day, so I'm partial to them. But we'll see. In any case, it looks like we can rule out Wade Townsend."

"He and Maya both seem to think that Lena is the killer. But we still have our meeting with Mac tonight. Even though he claims that he has evidence to clear his name, I won't believe it until I see it," Anna said.

"So, we're back to Maya, Lena, Chet, or Mac."

"Unless we get a break in the case, it looks like it could still remain unsolved when I return to Seagull Cove on Saturday."

"You know as well as I do that a lot can happen in a few days," Cassie said. "But even if we don't solve it, it's been fun working on a case together again this week. I should have known better than to think we would just hang out and relax."

"Sleuthing is definitely more on brand for us. Plus, I've loved seeing you live your new life in Sand Dune Shores now that you know your identity." Anna glanced at her phone. "It's almost 11:00. I should check out of the inn and move my things to your house."

The women returned to the inn, and Cassie checked Anna out while she packed her bag. Then they collected Artie and went to the beach house. It was sunny, so they decided to take him for another walk along the beach.

They paused as they turned past the dune.

"Every time I pass this dune, I can't help but think of Darren," Anna said solemnly.

"I know." Cassie thought back to their conversation with him on Monday afternoon. "From here, we know he likely went straight back to his studio, because Sydney's mom saw him there not long after he left the beach with his driftwood. There wouldn't have been enough time for him to go anywhere in between."

"And we know he was murdered in his showroom. Someone either brought the sharpened stake there to kill him or used a piece of wood from his studio."

Cassie shivered. "Imagine making your own murder weapon?"

"It truly is a new level of cruel to kill someone with their own art. The more I think about it, the more it feels like a very personal murder. The killer had to have strong feelings about him. Even if the killer brought the weapon, he or she chose to do it with driftwood. Talk about cold."

"Maybe we need to focus on who had strong enough feelings against Darren, not just to kill him, but to kill him with a piece of driftwood," Cassie said.

"Maya was very passionate about protecting the environment."

"True. And we don't know if Mac was being completely honest with us. They could have had a disagreement that went deeper than Mac was letting on. For all we know, he could have been lying to us about everything," Cassie said.

Artie pulled on his leash, so the women continued walking.

"That's true," Anna said. "He could have come to town specifically to kill Darren. But why would he have been staying with Darren? If they were bitter enemies, he would have stayed somewhere else. He didn't make the reservation to the inn until after Darren died, and Darren did say that he had a houseguest."

"Unless Mac hid his true feelings," Cassie said. "Maybe he had a plan all along but was playing it cool."

"It will be interesting to hear what he has to say tonight," Anna said.

"That still leaves Lena and Chet. It doesn't seem like Chet was angry enough at him to kill him in such a brutal manner."

"Not that we know of," Anna said. "But Lena could have been."

When they reached the small inlet that stopped them from going any further, they turned around and walked back to the beach house. "I need a break from sleuthing. How about lunch? I bought a broccoli and cheese quiche from a local farmstead."

"Sounds perfect."

Cassie warmed two slices of quiche and put them on some plates along with some potato chips, and they ate on the deck. The sun was strong, but there was a cool breeze coming off the ocean. She imagined the beach a month from now, with tourists and summer residents swarming about and the sound of children playing. She couldn't wait for her first summer at the beach house to begin. She had always wanted to live closer to the ocean, and she couldn't possibly be any closer.

"Let's just hang out here until we meet Mac tonight," Cassie suggested.

"You won't hear any arguments from me."

The women spent the afternoon enjoying the sunshine and chatting. They ordered a pizza for dinner and at 6:30, they went over to the inn.

"We told Mac that we'd meet him in the library at 7:00. Let's wait there so we don't miss him."

Jake popped in to confirm that he and Cassie planned to head to the docks the following morning to hopefully talk to Leo. Then he left to grab a quick bite to eat in the tavern before returning to work.

Artie hopped onto Cassie's lap, and they settled in. Then they waited. And waited.

Anna pulled her phone from her pocket. "It's 7:15. Do you think he's blowing us off?"

"Let's give him a few more minutes. Maybe he's running late."

Ten minutes later, there was still no sign of Mac.

"We should check to see if anyone else has seen him," Cassie said. "But I have a feeling he's going to be a no-show."

"I'll stay here in case he comes," Anna said.

Cassie stepped outside to the parking lot, but Mac's car wasn't there. Then she went to the office behind the tavern and checked the reservations. He hadn't checked out.

Joel walked into the office from the door that led to his and Elizabeth's private residence.

"Joel, have you seen Mac Dalton?" She asked.

"He's the guy that came here after Darren's murder, right?"

"That's the one."

"I haven't seen him since lunch this afternoon. Why? Wait, don't tell me. It's connected to your investigation, isn't it? Elizabeth told me that you and Anna were looking into his death."

Cassie nodded. "He was supposed to meet us tonight, but he didn't show up."

"He didn't exactly seem like the social type, but I figured it was because he just lost his friend. He spent most of the past few days holed up in his room."

"Did he mention anything about checking out early?"

"No. I'm sure he'll be back though if he hasn't checked out already. Maybe he forgot about your meeting. He does have a lot on his mind."

Cassie doubted that. She considered going upstairs to Mac's room to see if he was there, but since his car wasn't in the parking lot, she didn't bother. Instead, she went back to the library to update Anna.

"I wonder if he skipped town without checking out," Anna said.

"It's possible, but he knows that we'd go to the police and tell them about the break-in, so I doubt he'd do that."

"Unless he is the killer, and he took advantage of the time we gave him to skip town."

"I hope not. I have an idea, though. I still have the key to my old room, where Mac is staying…"

"I'm picking up what you're putting down," Anna said. "Let's go."

CHAPTER 16

Cassie fished the key to her old room from the bottom of her purse, and she and Anna went upstairs to search Mac's room.

"Are you sure you want to do this?" Anna asked. "Couldn't you get in trouble?"

"Considering he blew us off when he was supposed to provide us with evidence that would clear his name, I think we're justified."

"Fair enough. We did catch him stealing art from Darren's showroom, so we need to know what's going on."

Cassie unlocked the door and opened it. The room was much cleaner than the last time they were in there. There were no more pizza boxes and beer bottles, and most of his clothes were put away.

"At least we know he didn't skip town," Anna said.

"This doesn't make sense. Why would he blow us off when we know where he's staying? I half expected to find an empty room."

"It could have taken longer than he anticipated to get the

evidence. Maybe he'll be back tonight with a logical explanation," Anna suggested.

"This puts us in a dilemma. Should we call Rick and tell him that we caught Mac stealing Darren's artwork, or should we give him the benefit of the doubt?"

"If we call Rick, we'll have to explain what we were doing at Darren's last night. But if we don't call him, Mac could get away with attempted robbery," Anna said. "The longer we wait, the more trouble we'll be in if we do eventually have to inform Rick."

"Maybe we should give him the rest of the night. But if he's not back by tomorrow morning, we need to call Rick."

"I suppose that's a good compromise," Anna said. "And while we're here, we might as well see if we can find anything that might tell us where he went."

"It's worth a try."

The women searched every square inch of the room but found nothing besides clothes and toiletries. When they finished, Cassie locked the door and they left.

"I'll come here tomorrow morning while you and Jake are at the docks and see if Mac is back," Anna said. "When you return, we can regroup."

"Sounds like a plan. It's starting to get late and I'm meeting Jake early, so we should probably get going."

They brought Artie for a walk, then went back to Cassie's house to watch a movie before turning in.

The following morning, Jake picked up Cassie at 7:00, and they drove to the docks. There were about ten men milling about. A man in a black t-shirt and jeans, who was carrying a box into a warehouse, stopped when he saw them.

"Are you lost?" he asked.

"We're looking for Leo. Is he working?"

The guy pointed to another man in a green flannel shirt, who was leaning against a chain linked fence and eating a granola bar.

"Good morning. I'm Jake Harding, and this is Cassie Monroe. Are you Leo?"

The man nodded. "Do I know you?"

"No, but I think you knew my friend, John Seewald," Cassie said. "We were supposed to meet with you a few months ago. Do you remember him?"

Leo's eyes widened. "How could I forget? The guy was so insistent on meeting with me, and then he didn't show up. I was annoyed until I watched the news the next day and saw that he died in a car accident."

"That's right," Cassie said. "I was in that car, too. I was supposed to be with him when he talked to you, but I was in the hospital. Had you ever met him before?"

"Never met the guy in my life. I'm not even sure why he wanted to talk to me. He called me out of the blue and pretty much begged me to meet with him. After he died, I did an internet search on him and found out he did time for armed robbery. I still have no idea what he wanted with me. Do you know?"

"Yes and no." Cassie explained how she knew John and that she had been trying to help him prove that he was framed. "He has a young son, Caleb, and he wanted to clear his name for his sake. I'll be honest, Leo. I hadn't been in touch with John for many years, and I was skeptical when he turned up on my doorstep. But I decided to believe in my old friend. I have knowledge of the art world, which was why he asked me to help. After John died, I decided to see this investigation through, for his family's sake. Do you have any idea why he believed you could help him?"

"The more I learn about this guy, the less sense it makes that he wanted to talk to me. I don't have any connection to the art world, and I don't know how he thought I could help him."

"John believed that the man who framed him might be living in this area. There have been several reported art thefts from local galleries in the past few months, and he believed that the real thief was behind them," Jake said.

"The thief would need to hide the art—at least for a while—if he stole it, right?" Leo asked.

"That's what we were thinking," Cassie said.

"And he wouldn't likely want it to be in his possession," Leo said.

"Right again," Jake said.

"That must be it then. A few months ago, I was working overtime here at the docks, and I discovered that part of this warehouse was being used to house stolen goods."

"What kind of stolen goods?"

"Believe it or not, it was art."

"I believe it," Cassie said. "So, you found the stolen paintings?"

"Not paintings. They were sculptures and tapestries that were connected to a robbery in Ohio. The police never figured out who stole them and stashed them in the warehouse, but they were returned to their rightful owners. The local newspaper published an article about it, and I was featured," Leo said proudly.

"If it's the same robber, this guy gets around," Jake said. "Des Moines, Ohio, and Cape Cod."

"And those are only the locations that we know of," Cassie said. "I'll bet John wanted to pick your brain to see if you knew of any other possible hiding spots in the area for artwork."

"If that's the case, I'm not sure I could have helped him much. It was just a fluke that I came upon that spot."

"Did you ever see anyone unusual loitering around here before that?"

"Nope. Never," Leo said.

"Have you ever heard of a man with the nickname Red?" Cassie asked.

"No. I'd remember that. Wait a minute. Did the thief have red hair? Is that why they called him Red?"

"We think so," Cassie said. "Have you ever seen him?"

"I did see a man with red hair poking around here one time. I asked him if I could help him, and he turned and disappeared. Do you think he could be the one who framed John?"

"It's possible," Jake said. "Can you describe the man?"

"No. It was during a cold spell last November. I remember because he was bundled up. It's freezing down here in the winter. I didn't pay attention because I didn't think anything of it. He just looked like a random guy who took a wrong turn."

"Would you be able to show us where the sculptures you found had been stored?"

"I'm afraid I can't. It's private property," Leo said. "Besides, it's not like the thief would store his goods in the same place twice."

"True," Cassie said. "But I still wish we could see the spot."

Leo looked around. "There are signs around the warehouse that say, 'No Trespassing.' But…"

"We're listening," Cassie said.

"You didn't hear this from me, but the third window from the right on the side of the building that is facing the parking lot is broken. The owner hasn't boarded it up yet, so you could get in through there. There's a hidden room down below to the left, and that's where I found the artwork. It's climatized so it would be a good spot to hide paintings. There's nobody here at night, but again, you didn't hear that from me."

"Thanks, Leo."

"I'd better get back to work. Good luck. I'm only telling you because I heard the desperation in John's voice, and I was sorry to hear what happened to him. I also have a son his age, so I can sympathize. If he was innocent, I hope you are able to prove it."

"Me, too," Cassie said, feeling some hope for the first time.

CHAPTER 17

"So, how do you feel about breaking into a warehouse at night to look for clues?" Cassie asked Jake as they drove back to the inn.

He turned to Cassie and smiled. "I rather enjoy these adventures with you. I'm good as long as Rick doesn't find out."

Cassie thought of the conversation she likely had to have with Rick about Mac Dalton. He wasn't going to be pleased to learn that she had been trespassing at Darren's. If he caught them in the warehouse, that would be two offenses in one week. She couldn't let that happen. "We'll be careful. Neither one of us needs Rick on our back."

"Amen to that."

Jake stopped the car in front of the inn. "I've got to get to work, but we can connect later to figure out a good time for our little breaking and entering date."

She blushed at the word date, and he laughed.

She went inside and found Anna sipping a coffee at one of the tables in the tavern.

Cassie got herself a cup and joined Anna. "I was just killing time until you got back. How'd it go at the docks?"

Cassie relayed the details.

"Ooh, a break in. Sounds like fun."

"You and Jake are the only people I know who would say that," Cassie said, laughing. "I'm not even sure that *I'd* say that."

Anna shrugged playfully. "It *could* be fun, especially with the right person."

"I hope it goes better than our attempt at Darren's," Cassie said.

"That wasn't a total disaster. We did catch Mac in the act of stealing. Speaking of Mac, I went upstairs and knocked on his door, but there was still no answer. And his car still isn't in the parking lot."

"That's what I was afraid of," Cassie said. "It looks like we'll have to call Rick and explain what happened on Wednesday night."

"We might as well get it over with. We'll call as soon as you finish your coffee."

Cassie lingered over her java, dreading the phone call she had to make to Rick. She brought their empty cups into the kitchen, and the women started toward the library, hoping to find some privacy. As they were leaving the tavern, the front door to the inn opened and a tired-looking Mac Dalton walked through the door holding a large steaming cup and a bag from *Bobbi's Brews*.

The women stopped in their tracks, then jumped in front of Mac so he couldn't go any further.

Cassie put her hand on her hips. "We waited for you for more than a half hour last night, but you never showed. What happened to this supposed evidence you had that would clear your name of murder?"

He looked around nervously. "Not so loud. I have a good explanation. Follow me."

Cassie was skeptical as they followed him to the library.

"So, you have the evidence?" Anna asked.

"One thing at a time," Mac said.

"Let's start with why you didn't show up last night," Cassie said.

"I didn't show up, because Detective Rick Blaney came knocking on my door a half hour before we were supposed to meet. I almost had a heart attack when I saw him. I thought you two had gone back on your word and told him about Wednesday night."

"We didn't. But you went back on yours by not showing up," Anna said.

"Let me finish explaining. Geez, patience isn't your strong suit, is it? So, Detective Blaney asked to speak with me, and I thought it was about Wednesday night. It's a good thing I didn't blurt anything out, because he didn't know anything about it."

Cassie breathed a sigh of relief. "So, he still doesn't know?"

"Of course not. Do you think *I* was going to tell him?"

"Then he came to question you about Darren's murder again," Anna said.

"Yes. Apparently, Lena, that wannabe artist that works at the coffee shop…" He held up his bag. "She told him she saw the two of us arguing, and he wanted to know what it was about."

"And what *was* the argument about?" Cassie asked. "And

don't tell us it was over the Red Sox. We didn't buy that the first time."

He took a deep breath. "Darren was trying to convince me that he owed me less money than he did. I was furious, especially since his business was so successful and he could afford to pay me back. He was just being petty. But why would I kill him? If I did, I wouldn't get *anything*."

"And the police believed you?" Cassie asked.

"They did when I showed them a copy of the cleared check that I gave Darren three years ago. I had even written 'personal loan' in the memo, thank goodness. When we left the coffee shop the morning he died, I told him I was going to produce that canceled check to prove how much he owed me. I didn't have my computer with me to do it online, so I went to the bank to get it. When I returned, he was already dead."

"Was this the evidence you were going to show us?" Cassie asked.

"Yes. I figured if I could prove that Darren owed me money, you'd see that he was worth more to me alive than dead." He pulled out a printout of a bank statement from three years ago. "See. This check was made out to Darren to help him start his business. He needed some seed money to lease the studio and a place to live and to carry him through the winter, while he created enough inventory to sell to the summer tourists."

Cassie and Anna examined the document. It looked legitimate.

"How do we know that Darren hadn't already paid you back?" Cassie asked.

"That's what Rick said. So, I agreed to show him all my bank statements to prove that there was no deposit for this amount, or anywhere near it. I was at the police station using one of their computers to access my bank statements online when we were supposed to meet last night."

"That doesn't prove anything," Cassie said. "You could have deposited it into another account."

"I also showed him an email exchange between Darren and me, where Darren admitted that he owed me money and that he was going to pay me back this week. I left to get breakfast this morning, and I was planning to leave you a message in the gift shop as soon as I got back. But I didn't have to because there you were in the foyer. If my evidence was good enough for the police, I figured it had to be good enough for you."

"I guess this gets you off the hook," Cassie said. At least they didn't have to explain Wednesday night to Rick.

"It's true that my name has been cleared, but I lost a friend and I'm still leaving town without my money. Not only did I lose the money I lent Darren, but I'm out the cost of this trip, too. Not to mention the aggravation and grief. I did give Lena a piece of my mind this morning, though, when I was getting my breakfast. If you ask me, she's hiding something."

"Why do you say that?" Cassie asked.

"Just a gut feeling. Plus, Detective Blaney told me that the murder weapon wasn't made at Darren's studio. They think the killer brought it with them. Apparently, nothing Darren was working on involved any stakes. And from what I hear, Lena has been dabbling in wood carving, so she has the tools."

"We heard the same thing," Cassie said.

CHAPTER 18

Cassie spent a few minutes in the gift shop, checking in on her staff before the women went back to the beach house. Since the sun was warming the air, they once again sat on the deck. Just as they were about to discuss their conversation with Mac, the doorbell rang. It was Sydney.

She followed Cassie back to the deck.

"I was just sitting at home and trying to think of a way to procrastinate, and I thought of the two of you," Sydney said with a smirk. "I remember that you were supposed to meet Mac last night, so I thought I'd come by to see if he was able to provide that evidence he was talking about."

They caught Sydney up to speed on everything that had happened last night and this morning.

"So, the bottom line is, he has proof that he didn't kill Darren," Sydney clarified.

"To sum it up, yes. Given how much money Darren owed Mac, it's highly unlikely he would kill him," Cassie said.

"What if Darren refused to pay? That could give Mac a motive."

"According to the email exchange between Mac and Darren, Darren had every intention of reimbursing him. I think it's safe to remove him from our list of suspects," Anna said.

"Besides, if they had been having a disagreement over the money, Mac wouldn't be staying with Darren. I agree that we can take him off the list," Cassie said.

"Who does that leave for suspects?" Sydney asked.

"We only have three remaining—Lena, Chet, and Maya," Cassie said.

"I think Lena is the most likely candidate at this point," Anna said. "And Chet is the least likely."

Cassie nodded. "I'd agree with that. Rick told Mac that the police believe the murder weapon wasn't carved by Darren but that it was made off-site and brought to his showroom."

"That means it was premeditated," Anna said.

"And since Lena has been dabbling in wood carving, that makes her the most likely suspect," Cassie added.

"How are you going to figure out which of them did it?" Sydney asked.

Cassie and Anna looked at one another and shrugged.

"I'm leaving Saturday, and I'm not convinced we're going to solve it by then," Anna said.

"At least we got to spend time sleuthing together, for old times' sake," Cassie said.

"True. And I can always help you from Seagull Cove. You can keep me posted by phone. If we get stuck, I can run the details by my cousin Connie, too. She lives in Florida, but she also has a knack for solving tough cases."

"I remember you telling me about her when I was in Seagull Cove. I hope I can meet her someday," Cassie said.

"Me, too," Anna said. "You'd love her. You both would. Maybe we can take a road trip to the Cape the next time she's in Massachusetts."

"That would be lovely," Sydney said. "I'd better get back to my office. I think I've procrastinated long enough. I'm sure I'll see you tomorrow before you leave, but I'll say goodbye now, just in case." She gave Anna a hug. "And for the record, I agree. You should relax and enjoy the rest of your time here."

"Thanks. That's the plan," Anna said.

After Sydney left, Cassie's phone pinged with a text from Jake.

My new hires are working out well, so I can leave work early tonight. Do you want to check out that warehouse?

"Jake wants to go to the warehouse tonight, but I'm going to tell him it's not a good night. I don't want to leave you on your last night here," Cassie said to Anna.

"Don't worry about me. I'll hang tight here with Artie while you're gone. I'm sure it won't take more than an hour or so, tops. I could use a quiet evening, anyway."

"You could come with," Cassie said.

"I think I'll sit this one out. We've already broken into Mac's room and Darren's showroom. That's enough mischief for one trip."

"Fair enough," Cassie said, while she replied to Jake's text. "Would you like some more iced tea?"

"Sure. I'll come inside and help pour."

Cassie looked through the kitchen window. "On second thought, the tea can wait. Look who's walking into the inn."

Anna peered over Cassie's shoulder. "Is that Lena?"

"It sure is. Let's go over and see what we can learn."

Cassie and Anna walked across the street and arrived in

the foyer just in time to watch Lena enter the tavern. She sat at a table with a man whose back was facing them.

"We can get a better view from inside the restaurant. Come on," Cassie said.

They sat at a table by the bar, where they were less likely to be spotted.

"The man looks familiar, but I can't place him."

"You're right," Cassie said.

The conversation between them became animated. After a few minutes, the man stood abruptly and marched out the door. But not before he turned enough for them to see his face.

"That's Chet Mercer," Cassie said. "I didn't know he and Lena knew each other."

"Let's go talk to her."

The women made a beeline for Lena's table. "Hi, Lena," Cassie said. "It's nice to see you here."

"Oh, hi," Lena said.

"Do you mind if we sit down?" Cassie asked.

"I'd rather…"

They sat down before she could protest.

"Was that Chet Mercer?" Cassie asked. "I didn't realize the two of you were friends."

"Oh, we're not exactly friends."

"It looked like you were having quite the disagreement," Anna said.

She paused as if she were trying to collect her thoughts. "Oh, that? I was just annoyed because I heard he was raising the dues for membership in the Chamber of Commerce. I hoped that I could reason with him, but no such luck. He's dead set on making it difficult for struggling artists to be a member."

Anna looked incredulously at Lena. "He seemed very upset when he left."

"He was just in a bad mood. He'll get over it," Lena said. She put a five-dollar bill on the table. "This is for the coffee. I won't be staying. I lost my appetite," she said, standing to leave.

"Before you go, could we ask you a couple of questions?" Cassie asked.

"I'm actually in a hurry. I have to get to work."

"But weren't you planning to have lunch with Chet?" Cassie asked.

"Fine. But I have a lot of other things I should be doing, so I can't spare much time."

"The police told us that Darren's killer brought the murder weapon to the crime scene. That means that the killer had the tools and know-how to fashion the weapon."

Lena's eyes darted between Cassie and Anna. "Are you accusing me of killing Darren?" Lena stood up. "I swear I didn't kill him. I'm not going to sit here and take this."

"Please, Lena. If you didn't do it, who else had the ability and the tools to make that weapon?" Cassie asked.

"How should I know? Anyone could have collected driftwood from the beach and carved a stake. All I know is that I didn't kill him. I really have to go."

She darted out of the restaurant before the women could protest.

"I guess that relationship is over." Cassie turned to find Rob carrying a drink tray.

"Oh, hi, Rob." Cassie handed him the five-dollar bill that

Lena had left on the table. "She left this for the coffee. What do you mean by their relationship is over?"

"Are you saying Lena and Chet were a couple?" Anna asked.

"I assumed they were. I've seen them in here a few times, and they looked pretty cozy."

"You mean, like they were dating?"

He nodded. "I saw them holding hands."

A patron motioned for Rob to come over. "Duty calls," he said as he dashed off.

"I don't believe that flimsy excuse about their lunch date being to discuss the dues for the Chamber of Commerce," Anna said.

"I don't, either. What if they are dating and they killed Darren together?"

"I hadn't considered the possibility of two killers, but it's possible," Anna said.

"We'll definitely have to consider it. They both had a motive. They could have been working together."

CHAPTER 19

Cassie and Anna left the inn and returned to Cassie's house.

"We still have more questions than answers about Darren's murder," Cassie said. "Let's follow our initial plan and forget about the case for the rest of the day."

"Works for me." They returned to the deck with a fresh glass of iced tea.

It was an unseasonably warm day for the month of May, and the sun was growing stronger.

"I don't know if she killed Darren with Chet or alone, but Lena is looking more and more guilty," Cassie said after a few minutes of silence.

Anna chuckled. "I can't let it go, either. And I agree. Of our remaining suspects—Lena, Chet, and Maya—Lena had the easiest access to a murder weapon."

"Unless she is being framed. Maybe the killer chose a stake as the murder weapon to frame Lena. She's a sculptor who was dabbling in driftwood art. The killer could have realized that the police would eventually figure out that the killer brought the murder weapon to Darren's, and that Lena had the tools to make it. I could see Maya doing that," Cassie said.

"Maya also had easy access to driftwood because she lives on the beach."

"Or even Chet could have framed Lena," Cassie said

"On the other hand, if Lena and Chet were dating, why would he frame her for murder?" Anna asked.

"He could have been playing her. It doesn't sound like they had been dating for long, if they were dating at all. We don't know for sure that they were." Cassie thought for a moment. "Hold on. I have an idea." She went into the house and returned with her laptop computer. "Artists usually have a website." She did an internet search, and Lena's website popped up. "Here's Lena's."

Anna scooted her chair closer, and Cassie turned the computer so they could both see the screen.

"Look," Anna said. "There's a section that says, 'Driftwood Art Coming Soon."

Cassie clicked on the text, and they were brought to a preview page with some of the pieces that Lena was working on. "It looks like she's highlighting garden sculptures."

"That makes sense. She is a sculptor. Those are cute," Anna said. "I like the sunshine ornament. I think she'll do well with those."

"This boat is cute, too." Cassie clicked on a picture of one of the products.

The women looked at a few more pictures, then they looked at each other.

"Are you thinking what I'm thinking?" Anna asked.

"Each garden sculpture comes with a stake to fasten it to

the ground. She probably has a pile of those stakes in her studio," Cassie said.

"I think that's a safe assumption. She would need one for every sculpture."

Cassie expanded one of the photos, enlarging the stake.

"It looks exactly like the one that killed Darren," Anna said.

"You're right. The image is burned in my head. But why wouldn't Lena remove these pictures from her website?" Cassie asked. "They link her right to the murder."

"Maybe she thought if she removed them, it would make her look guilty. I wish we knew about this when we talked to her earlier. But then again, she would probably have claimed it was a coincidence."

"Besides, if her decision to kill Darren was an impulsive one, she wouldn't have had time to change her website. Then again, if she's innocent, she wouldn't have removed them because she wouldn't have had anything to hide. It's still circumstantial evidence," Cassie said.

"It may be circumstantial, but it's the only evidence we've found connecting anyone to the murder weapon," Anna said.

"When all is said and done, we're still back to the same three suspects. Although Lena is looking more and more guilty."

"There's not much we can do right now. What time is Jake picking you up for your exploration of the warehouse?"

"Not until 8:00. We want to make sure it's dark and empty."

"In that case, do you want to go out to eat tonight? My treat to thank you for letting me stay at this amazing beach house."

"I'd love to," Cassie said. "But I insist on paying. You have done so much more for me than I could ever repay. If you don't let me pay, I won't go."

Anna laughed at Cassie's dramatics. "Well, I don't want to eat alone…"

After another leisurely walk on the beach with Artie, they returned to the beach house. "I know the perfect restaurant by the water where we can go," Cassie said. "It has a beautiful dining room with large windows overlooking the ocean."

"That sounds lovely," Anna said.

The women showered and changed, then left for dinner.

Since it was still early, there were plenty of available tables, so they were able to choose one next to a window. The calm water helped Cassie to take her mind off things.

"Everything looks delicious," Anna said.

"This was one of the first restaurants I went to with Sydney and Jake when I got my bank account back. I wanted to thank them for everything they had done for me and my cooking isn't the greatest, so I found this place online. They buy their seafood straight from the docks."

When the server returned, Cassie ordered grilled salmon and Anna ordered baked stuffed shrimp. When they were halfway through their meal, Chet entered the restaurant with an attractive woman. The hostess sat them a few tables over.

When he noticed Cassie and Anna staring, he gave them an uncomfortable wave. Then he quickly turned his attention back to his dinner companion.

"I wish we could hear their conversation," Cassie said.

"I know. They're just out of earshot. How annoying," Anna said.

"Do you think they're on a date?"

"It's hard to tell. They could just be…"

Before Anna could get the sentence out, Chet reached for the woman's hand and smiled.

"On second thought, it does look like a date," Anna said.

"I suppose if his relationship with Lena is new, they may not be exclusive."

Chet glanced nervously at the women.

"We have to stop staring," Cassie said. "We're being too obvious."

"You're right. But it's hard to look away."

The women returned their attention to their meals. Cassie glanced over at the couple from time to time, but looked away before Chet could notice.

When they finished their meals, the server returned. "Can I get you anything else?"

"How about dessert?" Cassie asked Anna.

"I shouldn't, but..."

"I'll give you a moment with the dessert menu."

"Thanks. I'll have a coffee to start with," Cassie said.

"Same," Anna said.

"I'm going to get a hot fudge sundae," Cassie said after perusing the menu.

"I think I'll have the fudge brownie. I eat enough ice cream in my shop."

The server returned with their coffees and took their dessert order. A few minutes later, she returned with two generously portioned desserts.

Just as they were about to dig in, Chet's date stood and walked toward the ladies' room.

To Cassie's surprise, Chet came over. "Hello, ladies. Those look good," he said, gesturing towards their desserts.

"They sure do," Cassie said.

"Have you given any more thought to renting out your extra unit?" Chet asked.

So, that was why he wasn't ignoring them.

"I probably won't do it this summer, but it's on the back-burner for another year."

"I see. Well, you know where to find me when you're ready," Chet said.

Cassie nodded. "I do. And thank you for your help. I was going to let you know this afternoon, when we saw you at the tavern with Lena. But you left too quickly."

"You sure do eat out a lot," Anna said.

"Well, I didn't exactly stay for lunch. Lena and I broke up, so there was no point in prolonging it."

"It looks like you made a quick rebound," Anna observed.

"Allie and I are better suited for each other. It was bound to happen. It's probably better for all of us that it ended sooner rather than later. Anyway, it was good to see you. Enjoy your dinner." He started to leave, then hesitantly turned around. "The last time I talked to you, you were investigating Darren's death. Have you made any progress?"

"I can't say that we have," Cassie said. She didn't exactly want to say that they had narrowed it down to three suspects, one of whom was Chet.

"Well, I'm sure the police will solve it soon. It's probably best to leave it to them, anyway."

"And focus on life's little pleasures," Cassie said, picking up a spoon to dig into her sundae, which was starting to melt.

"Cheers to that. I'll leave you to your dessert. Enjoy, ladies."

"What do you think that was all about?" Cassie asked after they savored the first few bites of their desserts.

"I don't know. Something doesn't sit right with me. Chet seemed angry at lunch. If they did break up, I don't think he's the one who broke up with Lena," Anna said.

"Although she seemed angry, too."

"Maybe she dumped him, and he wanted to save his pride in front of us."

"Could be," Anna said. "It seems that everyone is acting strangely, and we keep going in circles. Let's just enjoy our desserts."

"No argument here."

Once they finished, they went back to Cassie's.

CHAPTER 20

Anna relaxed on the recliner and found a cozy mystery on TV while Cassie changed for her meeting with Jake. Ten minutes later, she emerged from her bedroom wearing black yoga pants, a black long-sleeved t-shirt, and black sneakers.

Anna laughed when she saw her. "You're certainly looking the part."

"Thanks… I think," Cassie said. She opened a nearby closet and retrieved a flashlight. "This should come in handy."

Cassie sat on the couch while she waited for Jake. "I see you're keeping your sleuthing skills sharp," she teased.

"You'd think with all the sleuthing I do in real life that I wouldn't want to watch mysteries on television, but I find them relaxing."

"You never know. Something could spark an idea for our case."

"I'll let you know," Anna said.

Cassie heard a vehicle pull into the driveway. "That sounds like Jake. I'll see you later."

"Be careful." Anna chuckled when the words came out of her mouth. "It's funny. I'm usually on the receiving end of that advice."

Cassie hopped into Jake's Wrangler.

"You look ready to sneak into a warehouse," he said. Jake was also dressed in dark clothes, but not in black from head to toe, like Cassie was.

"I'm as ready as I'll ever be."

They once again drove to the docks, and Jake parked in a dark corner of the parking lot under a tree. "I don't think anyone will see my car from the road."

They got out of the vehicle and headed toward the warehouse, making their way to the side where Leo had told them the broken window was located. "Here it is," Cassie said. "Leo was right. There's a large enough opening for us to fit through."

They passed through the window and entered a vast, mostly empty warehouse.

"I didn't realize how damp it would be," Cassie said. "I can't see how anyone could have stored valuable paintings in here."

"Leo said that the hidden room was climatized." Jake pointed to a corner of the warehouse. "He said it was in the corner, didn't he?"

"I think so."

They went to the back corner closest to the street, but there was no sign of a hidden door. Then they walked the perimeter of the warehouse, and when they arrived at the corner closest to the docks, Cassie noticed that the ground was uneven. So, she stomped on it. "This part of the floor is made of wood. It must be what we're looking for."

Jake came over and stooped down to examine what they hoped was the hidden door. He found a handle and yanked on it until a staircase appeared.

"Let's check it out," Cassie said.

Jake glanced around. "Maybe we both shouldn't go down there at the same time. What if someone happens upon us and closes the door? Nobody would be able to find us."

"Well, Anna would get worried sooner or later, but we don't want to be stuck in here until she does. You stay up here and let me know if anyone is coming."

Cassie climbed down the stairs and turned on her flashlight.

"Do you see anything?" Jake called down after a few minutes.

"I don't know. Hold on."

When she shined her flashlight around the space, she saw that it looked much like the warehouse above, except smaller. Until she noticed a room to her left. She walked over and pushed open the door.

"I think I found something," she called up to Jake.

She heard him descend the staircase, and he joined her in the room, which looked to be about two hundred square feet. There was a mahogany desk in the corner on top of mauve carpet. The wallpaper was floral.

"It looks like an office," Jake said.

"One that hasn't been used in a while. It's dusty and judging from the decor, it looks like it was decorated in the 1990s." Cassie walked over to the desk and opened the drawers. They're empty."

Jake turned on the overhead florescent lights. "At least the lights work. This must be the room where Leo discovered the sculptures and tapestries."

They examined every square inch of the room, but there was no sign of anything unusual.

"I'm not even sure what we're looking for," Jake said.

"Me, either. But it does look like a room where paintings could be stored. It has both heat and air conditioning."

"But there's no proof that there were actual paintings stored here," Jake said. "This is beginning to feel pointless."

"Wait a minute," Cassie said. "There's another door." On the other side was a large, empty walk-in closet.

Jake followed her inside. "What's that?" he asked, pointing to the back corner of the closet.

Cassie got on her hands and knees and touched a small piece of white fabric. "These look like small pieces of a canvas."

There was a roll of brown paper on one of the shelves.

"This could have been used to wrap and store paintings," Cassie said. Then she noticed some color on the threshold of the closet door. "Is that paint?"

Cassie took out her phone and snapped pictures of everything. Then she went to the threshold and ran her fingers across a dried blue substance.

"I think so. It looks like there may have been some paintings recently stored in here. But Leo said he didn't find any paintings."

"They could have been removed before he discovered the room."

Suddenly, a rattling sound came from upstairs. Before Cassie knew it, she had thrown her arms around Jake's waist, burying her head against his chest.

He immediately wrapped his arms around her in return.

She pried herself away. "I'm sorry, Jake. That sound scared me half to death."

He brushed back the hair that had fallen in front of her eyes and smiled. "I'm not."

He leaned forward, but another rattling noise echoed from above.

Jake turned off the lights and closed the door behind them, plunging the office into darkness. He took Cassie's hand, and they both flew out of the office and bolted toward the stairs.

"I think it was just the wind. But let's get out of here, anyway."

"You don't have to ask me twice. This place is creepy, and we found what we came for."

"We did. John's suspicions might have been right. It's at least possible that Red stored some paintings here. It can't be a coincidence that John was interested in this place and that we found traces of canvas, paint, and brown wrapping paper."

"I agree. Let's get back to my house. I can't think straight here with this howling wind."

CHAPTER 21

As Cassie and Jake drove back to her beach house, she debated whether to bring up the almost-kiss. In the end, she decided to let the conversation happen naturally, when the time was right.

When they got back, Anna was hanging up Artie's leash after bringing him for his nightly walk.

"Thanks for doing that, Anna," Cassie said.

Anna scratched the top of Artie's head. "It's the least I could do. Artie and I had a great time hanging out and watching a movie. But forget about us. How did your night go?"

They told Anna about the room that they found beneath the trap door in the warehouse and the traces of paint and canvas that were inside the back closet.

Cassie sat next to Anna, pulled out her phone, and tapped on the screen. "I took these photos."

Anna swiped through them and expanded the photos of the paint and canvas bits. "I mean, I think it's safe to say that there were paintings stored there. But we can't be sure if they were connected to this Red character or if they are even the same paintings that were stolen from the galleries and museums."

"That's true," Cassie said. "But it's a start. Since John's first stop in Sand Dune Shores was supposed to be to talk to Leo at the docks, it can't be a coincidence. And don't forget that the items that Leo found turned out to be stolen. There could very well be a connection."

Anna smiled at Cassie and Jake. "My money is on you two."

"It will be interesting to hear what Aunt Trudy learns when she speaks with the other gallery owners," Jake said.

The three of them chatted for a while before Jake headed home.

"Can you stay for the whole day tomorrow, or are you in a rush to get back to Seagull Cove?"

"I'm not in any rush. My staff isn't expecting me back at work until Sunday."

"Perfect. Then we can have dinner here. I have some burgers we can put on the grill. What else do you want to do on your last day in town?" Cassie asked.

"I'm good with just enjoying the beach and this sweet little puppy. The rest and the change of scenery have been good for me. Although..."

Cassie finished her sentence. "Although you're still thinking about Darren's murder."

Anna sat cross-legged on the couch. "I feel like we've been dancing all around the solution to this mystery, but nothing seems to fit."

"I know what you mean," Cassie said. "We keep going back to the same three suspects. We know Lena is creating driftwood garden sculptures that require stakes, just like the one Darren was murdered with."

"And Chet was angry with Lena at the tavern," Anna added. "He could have realized that she's the killer and confronted her. Maybe that's why they broke up and he moved on so quickly."

"Of course, Lena could have broken up with Chet because she figured out that he is the killer," Cassie said.

"And then there's Maya. She has the strongest motive, and Sydney's mom saw her at Darren's the afternoon he was killed."

"Even though she's not a sculptor, she could have carved the murder weapon. She has easy access to plenty of driftwood, and she did say it was poetic justice that he was killed that way. If anyone had a motive, it was Maya. It would be the perfect way to get back at Darren."

"I wouldn't mind talking to one more person before I leave tomorrow," Anna said.

"Who did you have in mind?"

"Chet," Anna said. "But we should be more direct with him than we were when we saw him in the restaurant earlier. Maybe if we press him, he will reveal something."

"We could go back to his office tomorrow morning," Cassie suggested.

"That sounds like a good plan. But only after a long walk on the beach. I don't want to waste my last morning here."

On Saturday morning, the women got up early, showered, and had a hearty breakfast of bacon and eggs. "This is one of the few things I know how to make well," Cassie joked as she scooped some scrambled eggs onto Anna's plate.

After breakfast, they loaded the dishwasher and walked

the beach in both directions before returning to the beach house an hour later.

"Shall we head to Chet's office?" Cassie asked after they had rehydrated.

"Let's go."

The women hopped into Cassie's car and before they knew it, they were back in the lobby of *Beachside Vacations*.

Chet glanced their way, then spun his chair so that his back was facing them. He motioned for another agent to approach him. When she did, he said something to her, then picked up his phone and proceeded to look busy.

The woman who had been talking with him came over to Cassie and Anna. "Hello, ladies, can I help you?"

"We were hoping to speak with Chet Mercer. We were working with him before."

"He's very busy today, but I'm sure I can help you. My name is Tracy. Are you looking to rent a property?"

"We'd rather speak with Chet. Is there another time we could come back?"

"I'm happy to help you. There's nothing that Chet could help you with that I can't," Tracy said.

"We'd really rather speak with Chet," Anna insisted.

Tracy let out an annoyed sigh and turned back towards Chet's desk. But his chair was empty.

"I don't think that's going to be possible. It looks like he just left."

"You mean, he slipped out the back door?" Cassie asked.

Tracy shrugged her shoulders. "He probably has a showing."

"Or he's trying to avoid us," Anna said.

Tracy looked uncomfortable. "I doubt that. I've never

known him to avoid a potential client. It's usually quite the opposite."

"Thank you for your time," Cassie said, realizing it was a losing battle. "We'll come back another time."

"He was obviously avoiding us," Anna said when they got back into Cassie's SUV. "What do you think that was all about?"

Cassie shrugged. "Guilty conscience?"

"Wait a minute," Anna said, peering through the passenger side window. "That woman looks familiar." She gestured toward a slight woman walking down the sidewalk towards Chet's office whose back was facing them.

"It looks like Lena," Cassie said.

"I think you're right."

Anna opened the door, and Cassie followed suit.

"Lena!" Anna cried out.

The woman sped up.

"Lena, we just wanted to talk for a minute," Cassie said.

The woman glanced over her shoulder. It was definitely Lena, but she didn't show any sign of slowing down. Instead, she raced across the street to honking horns and slamming brakes, and sprinted to a car a short distance away. Then she sped off.

CHAPTER 22

Cassie and Anna got back into Cassie's car, but they were too late to follow Lena. Her car was already out of sight.

"Well, that was strange," Anna said.

"I'll say. Chet and Lena completely blew us off. I'm really starting to think they worked together to kill Darren."

"It's sure looking that way," Anna said. "First, we find out they're dating. Then, we see them arguing at the *Sand Dune Tavern,* and later, Chet claims they broke up."

"And this morning, Lena was obviously on her way to see Chet. I doubt it was about a vacation rental," Cassie added.

"I suppose they could have gotten back together, but that wouldn't explain why they are both avoiding us like the plague. Lena couldn't get away from us fast enough, and Chet disappeared out the back door."

"Maybe they didn't actually break up when we saw them at the tavern. Maybe they were arguing because of the stress of having committed murder together," Cassie said. "Although

Chet did seem to have moved on when we saw him at the restaurant with a date."

"Maybe they broke up because the stress of committing murder was getting to them. Or maybe they disagreed on what to do next. Why else would they both be avoiding us while still trying to meet up with each other? It has to be connected to the murder."

"Something's not right. How are we going to figure out what?" Cassie asked.

Cassie's cell phone rang, startling the women. "It's Jake," she said, accepting the call. "Hi, Jake."

"Are you busy right now?" he asked.

"Nope. We just tried to talk to Chet, but he wanted no part of us. Then we saw Lena and tried to talk to her, but she ran in the opposite direction. So, we're headed back to my house."

"Can you meet me at the inn?" he asked. "I have something I'd like to run by you."

"Does it have anything to do with Darren's case?" Cassie asked.

"No. It's about Red."

"Alright," Cassie said. "We're headed there now."

"Since it's not connected to Darren's case, I think I'll wait for you at the beach house," Anna said. "I still need to pack. That way, when you're done with Jake, we can enjoy the rest of the day."

When Cassie got to the inn, Jake was sipping a cup of coffee in the tavern. Cassie poured one for herself, and they went into the sunroom to talk.

"What's going on, Jake?" she asked, taking a chair that was away from the direct sunlight.

"I called Trudy to let her know what we found when we snuck into the warehouse the other night."

"Are you sure it was a good idea to tell her about that?" Cassie asked.

"She's one hundred percent trustworthy, if that's what you mean. And I don't see how it's putting her in any danger. In fact, the more she knows, the safer she'll be."

"I suppose you're right."

"Anyway," Jake continued, "she's been asking around, but I promise, she's being discreet. One of her colleagues, Sue, found a letter on the floor of her gallery around the time some paintings were stolen. She thought it belonged to a customer, but Trudy wonders if it could have been from Red. The letter just said, 'Game on,' and was signed 'R.' What's really unsettling is that it was written on a notepad with her gallery's logo. When she asked her employees about it, one of them, Kerri, remembered a man with red hair and bright blue eyes browsing paintings one afternoon. He asked her for a piece of paper and a pen, and she gave them to him, thinking he wanted to write down the name of a painting he liked. Sue didn't tell Kerri who she suspected the man really was, but she did tell Trudy."

"Does Sue still have the letter?"

"Unfortunately, Kerri threw it away, because it looked like trash. It didn't even occur to her that it could belong to the person who robbed the gallery."

"But you said that Kerri remembers what the man looks like?" Cassie asked.

Jake nodded. "That's why I wanted to tell you right away. I figured that with your experience as a sketch artist, maybe you could sketch him from her description."

"That's a great idea. Can you arrange it?" Cassie asked.

"I'll call Aunt Trudy and ask her to find out if Kerri would be willing to meet with you to sketch the man. At least it would give us an idea of who we're looking for."

"Perfect," Cassie said. "Just let me know when, and I'll be there."

Jake left to go back to work, and Cassie checked in on her staff before leaving. By the time she got back to her beach house, Anna had already packed. Cassie told her about her conversation with Jake.

"That's fantastic," Anna said. "It looks like John Seewald's instinct was right. Your experience as a sketch artist could come in handy."

A warm feeling came over Cassie. She just might be able to help her old friend, after all.

"It's almost lunchtime, and the sun is shining. Would you like to grab some sandwiches and eat outside?"

"Sounds perfect," Anna said.

The women drove to a weathered wooden building that looked more like a shack than a restaurant. "It doesn't look like much, but they make their bread fresh every day, and they source their ingredients locally when they can."

Cassie ordered a turkey sandwich on wheat bread with a cranberry and mayo spread, and Anna got a chicken sandwich with avocado. They each bought a bottle of water and sat at a picnic table overlooking the ocean.

"I hate to leave without solving Darren's case," Anna said. "It seems like we're close, but it looks like you'll need another sidekick to finish this one out."

"Maybe I can convince Sydney," Cassie said.

"If only there was a way to talk to Lena and Chet again. But I don't see how after what happened this morning."

"We could go to the coffee shop where Lena works, but I feel like that wouldn't end well," Cassie said.

When they finished their sandwiches, they went back to the inn to get Artie. They were about to leave when Cassie's arm flew out in front of Anna. She couldn't believe her eyes when she saw Lena eating in the tavern.

CHAPTER 23

Lena stood when she spotted Cassie and Anna. Cassie braced for another runaway suspect, but instead of running, Lena nervously walked in their direction.

"I have to admit, I'm more than a little surprised to see you here," Cassie said.

"Especially after you ran away from us this morning when we tried to talk to you," Anna added.

Lena's gaze fell to the ground. "I was afraid that Chet would see me talking to you."

"I don't understand," Cassie said. "Why would that matter?"

"After I fled from you this morning, I went back to Chet's office to confront him, but he wasn't there. None of his co-workers knew where he was. He lives in that office, especially during this time of year. I hate to admit it because I really had strong feelings for him, and I don't want to believe that I could have fallen for a criminal. But I think he's hiding something."

A stream of people came into the tavern. "Can we go somewhere more private to talk?" Lena asked.

Cassie glanced at Anna, unsure of whether they should trust her. Anna seemed to share her skepticism.

"Sure. Let's go to the sunroom," Cassie said.

"What makes you think you can't trust Chet?" Anna asked after they sat down.

"I think Chet killed Darren. Actually, I'm terrified that he did."

"Why do you think that?" Cassie asked.

She looked at the floor, apparently contemplating whether she should trust them.

"You can tell us," Cassie said. "One way or another, the truth will come out."

"I was sanding some driftwood a few days ago and when I finished, I took an inventory of my garden sculptures. That's when I noticed that one of my stakes was missing. I specifically remember carving twelve stakes, and now there are only eleven."

"And you think that Chet took it?"

"I create all my art in my garage—at least until I can afford a proper studio. Chet is the only one who has a key to my house, besides my mother, and she wouldn't hurt a fly."

Cassie was just thinking that perhaps Lena's mother had the same motive as Lena.

Lena seemed to read her mind. "I know what you're thinking, but my mother wasn't even in town when Darren was killed. She was in Aruba with friends."

Cassie wasn't sure if she believed Lena, or if she was just throwing Chet under the bus. "You should go to the police with your suspicions," she said.

"Are you kidding? And tell them that I'm missing a driftwood stake? No way! They'll never believe me."

"You do have a point," Cassie said. "Did you manage to find Chet this morning after you left his office?"

Lena shook her head. "I texted him and told him I wanted to talk to him, but he didn't get back to me. I need to confront him about the missing stake."

"Well, if he did take it, he probably knows that you won't go to the police, since it would make you look guilty. So he may not be in a rush to get back to you," Cassie said. She wanted Lena to feel like they were on her side.

"Is that why you broke up with him?" Anna asked. "Because you noticed the missing stake?"

"Things had been going so well between us before that, but once I put the pieces together, I couldn't end it fast enough. He seemed surprised when I broke up with him, so I don't think he realized I was on to him. But by now, he must know I figured it out. Why else would he be avoiding me?" Lena glanced at the clock. "I want to get home and do some sculpting. I need to calm myself down. Working in my garage studio always helps. I even called in sick today so I could be alone."

"I understand," Cassie said. "Painting does the same for me. Let us know if you talk to Chet. And if you confront him, make sure it's in a public place." She wasn't sure if she believed Lena's story, but if she *was* telling the truth, the young woman could be in danger.

Lena nodded. "Alright."

"Do you think she was telling the truth?" Cassie asked Anna after Lena left. "Or do you think she was trying to frame Chet?"

"She did look scared, but it could be an act. The fact

remains that the murder weapon came from her garage. She probably knows that it's only a matter of time until the police discover that," Anna said.

"I suppose you're right." Cassie picked up the empty coffee cups from the coffee table. "I'm going to bring these back to the kitchen. Then we can decide what we want to do for the rest of the afternoon."

Anna followed her, and as they left the tavern, Chet stood in the doorway, craning his neck as he scanned the restaurant.

Cassie and Anna darted toward him.

His shoulders fell when he saw the women. "Hi, ladies. Um, I'm sorry I couldn't talk earlier. A work emergency came up."

Cassie wasn't buying it.

"I'm looking for Lena," he said. "She texted me earlier that she was trying to connect. She said she was coming here for lunch." He glanced nervously around the tavern again.

"She was here, but she's gone now," Anna said.

"Do you know where she went?" he asked.

"She didn't say." Cassie didn't want to give away that Lena would likely be alone working in her garage.

He started to say something, but then he stopped.

"What is it?" Cassie asked.

Chet took a deep breath, and his eyes grew misty.

"It's okay. You can trust us. Maybe we can help," Anna said.

People were passing them on their way to the tavern. "Come on. Let's talk in the library."

They sat on the soft leather couches.

"I suspect that Lena might have murdered Darren," he blurted out. "I came here to confront her. It's driving me crazy to not know the truth."

Cassie and Anna exchanged a confused glance. "Why do you think that?"

"She's been behaving so strangely. She started acting really nervous around me a few days ago. Then, she broke up with me when things were going fine between us. She must have figured out that I'd realize the murder weapon came from her garage. I only figured it out last night. That's why I ran away from you this morning. I wasn't ready to admit it to anyone. I don't know what to do. I don't want to rat out my girlfriend. Or ex-girlfriend. And I don't know for sure that she even is guilty. But I can't think of another reason for her strange behavior, and the murder weapon did come from her garage. It had to have. I saw a box of identical stakes the last time I was there. I had forgotten, but then I pieced it all together."

Cassie studied Chet. He seemed earnest. "There is another reason she may have been acting strangely."

His eyes widened with hope. "Why? Please tell me."

"Because she knows that you have a key to her place. If she knows that *she* didn't kill Darren, she might suspect that *you* did," Cassie said.

Chet looked at them in stunned silence. "Did she tell you that?"

Cassie nodded. Confronting him with this information was the only way to get to the bottom of things.

"Oh, my goodness. That *would* explain her strange behavior. But I swear, I didn't kill Darren."

"For the sake of argument, if neither you nor Lena killed him, then who did?" Anna asked. "Who else had access to Lena's garage?"

All of a sudden, Cassie recalled their conversation with

Maya about her dropping off driftwood at Lena's house a few weeks ago.

"Maya," she and Chet said at the same time.

"You're right," Anna said. "Maya told us that she collected a pile of driftwood for Lena and left it in her garage. That means she knew where the spare key was located. She must have seen the wooden stakes and decided to kill Darren with tools from his own craft."

"I have to talk to Lena right away," Chet said with both relief and fear in his voice. "I can't bear the thought that she thinks I'm a killer. I never should have doubted her."

"We weren't being truthful with you earlier when we said that we didn't know where she was because we didn't know if we could trust you. She called in sick to work today. She's at home sculpting in her garage."

"We'll go with you," Cassie said. "After that, the four of us can go to the police together."

"Alright," Chet said. "The sooner Maya is behind bars, the better."

CHAPTER 24

They took two cars to Lena's house. When they exited their respective vehicles, Cassie noticed movement through the living room window. "It looks like she's in the living room. She must have changed her mind about sculpting in the garage."

"I can't wait to tell her about this misunderstanding," Chet said. "I feel so foolish for jumping to conclusions." He started toward the front door, then stopped and turned toward the driveway. "I just realized there are two cars in the driveway. One is Lena's, but I don't recognize the Lexus."

Someone pulled down the shades to the living room window.

"Oh, no. Do you think she saw me and she's afraid to talk to me?" Chet asked.

"Let's go together. We'll tell her you're with us and that everything is okay."

When they got to the door, Cassie rang the doorbell.

"It's not a good time," Lena said through the door after a couple of minutes.

"Lena, it's Cassie and Anna. We have some good news for you. Can you let us in?" Cassie asked.

There was another pause. "I'm sorry, but you'll have to come back later. I can't talk right now."

Cassie thought she heard another voice coming from inside. It sounded as if someone had barked an order at Lena.

"Please come back later. All of you."

"I don't like the tone of her voice," Chet said. "She sounds scared."

He banged three times on the door with the palm of his hand. "Lena, let us in now. We're not going to leave until we see that you're okay."

Chet raised his hand to start pounding on the door again, but Lena slowly opened it. Chet pushed his way in, and Cassie and Anna followed. It wasn't until after Lena threw her arms around Chet's waist and began sobbing that Cassie noticed Maya in the living room wielding a gun.

"Everyone in the corner," Maya yelled.

"I'm sorry," Lena said between sobs. "I tried to tell you not to come in."

Cassie noticed a small pile of driftwood on the floor and understood what must have happened. "Maya came over to bring you some more driftwood and that's when you realized that she was the killer. Am I right?"

Lena nodded. "I'm sorry that I suspected you, Chet. It wasn't until she showed up at my door with the wood that I remembered she knew how to get into my house. I told her where the spare key was hidden when she delivered the first batch of driftwood to me."

"So, that's when you saw the pile of sharpened stakes in the garage and realized they'd make the perfect murder weapon. You stole one and used it to kill Darren," Cassie said to Maya.

"You figured you would teach Darren a lesson by killing him with a piece of driftwood. It was some sort of sick revenge for climbing on the dunes to collect his wood," Anna added.

"He had it coming," Maya said. "He came to Sand Dune Shores as an outsider and threatened our fragile beach ecosystem by trampling on the dunes. He cared more about making money from his art than about our community. He didn't deserve to live here. Or anywhere else, for that matter."

"And you came here today, because you knew it was only a matter of time before Lena realized that you were one of the few people who had access to her wood," Cassie said.

"You know, I'm glad you are all here. The police don't seem to suspect me, but I knew that it was only a matter of time until you figured it out. You just wouldn't stop asking questions." She looked at Chet. "It is, however, unfortunate that you showed up with these women. For both of us."

"Be serious, Maya," Cassie said. "You can't kill us all. The police are going to figure it out if we all disappear."

"I'm not going to kill you. At least, not if you cooperate. Here's what's going to happen. Lena's going to get me some rope, and I'm going to tie you up. Then I'm going to drive across the border, where my unsuspecting sister is waiting for me. Once I'm out of the country, there will be nothing the police can do, even if they figure out where I am. I'll take Lena with me as insurance."

"Take me instead," Chet said.

"Not happening. Lena will be easier to control. You might overpower me. Go, Lena! I know you have a rope in your garage. I saw it when I was getting the stake. Don't you dare try anything funny, or your friends will pay."

Cassie was glad that Chet was with them. She wasn't sure if Anna's and her safety alone would be enough incentive to stop Lena from taking off.

Lena looked at Chet nervously, and he nodded.

"Do what she says. It's our only chance. This will all be over soon," he said.

But judging from the traumatized look in Lena's eyes, she was realizing that the worst could be yet to come for her.

Cassie and Anna glanced at each other. Cassie didn't have any ideas on how to stop Maya from leaving with Lena, and judging from her expression, it didn't look as though Anna did either.

A few minutes later, Lena still hadn't returned. Just when Cassie was starting to believe Lena had ditched them all, she returned with a pile of rope in her trembling arms.

Maya shoved the rope at Anna. "Tie him up," she said, gesturing with her head toward Chet. "Tie him to the banister."

There was a black wrought-iron railing on a staircase leading upstairs, through which Cassie could see the dining room. Unfortunately, it looked pretty solid.

Anna brought Chet to the staircase. He sat on the first step while Anna tied him up. Maya inspected her work. "That won't do. Tighten the rope."

Anna did as she was told, giving Chet an apologetic look.

While they all watched Anna bind his hands, Cassie noticed a driftwood sculpture sitting on the dining room table in the next room.

"Cassie next," Maya barked.

Cassie reluctantly walked toward the staircase. Her back was facing Maya, so she gestured with her eyes toward the garden sculpture. She was trying to figure out if there was any way to use it to escape their current situation.

Chet seemed to catch on to Cassie's idea, but his hands were bound, so she couldn't count on his help.

Suddenly, Chet began squirming, as if trying to break loose.

"Stop that, Chet," Maya cried out.

"I won't let you take Lena," he said, continuing to make a commotion.

"Stop it, or you'll regret it." Maya reached for Lena, but she evaded her.

"I said stop it!" Maya raised the gun and stepped toward the staircase.

Lena looked as if she were considering her options.

Cassie attempted to get the driftwood so she could use it to take a swing at Maya, but she knocked it over before she could grab it, causing a loud bang as it hit the floor. Anna took advantage of the distraction to slip some of the remaining rope around Maya's neck, which caused her to drop the gun. Cassie sprinted back to the staircase and snatched it from the ground in front of Maya, while Lena untied Chet's hands and the two embraced.

Then Anna tied Maya up in the spot that Chet had previously occupied while Cassie called 9-1-1.

CHAPTER 25

The police arrived a few minutes later, and Rick wasn't far behind. A police officer took Maya away while Cassie, Anna, Lena, and Chet explained to Rick everything that had happened. Then they went to the police station to give their official statements.

An hour later, the four of them walked out of the police station together, with Chet and Lena holding hands.

"We can't thank you enough for all you've done for us," Chet said. "Not only did you find Darren's killer and clear both our names, but you gave us our relationship back."

"I can't believe we suspected each other of murder," Lena said. "I guess it would be an understatement to say that our relationship didn't get off to the best start."

"At least we'll have a good story to tell our grandkids," Chet said, smiling sheepishly at Lena, who was blushing.

"I mean, we could one day," he quickly added. "You never know what life has in store."

She returned his smile. "It would be an epic story."

Chet put his arm around Lena's shoulders, "Let's celebrate. How about dinner?"

"As long as we finish it off with a slice of chocolate cake. I need something sweet to calm my nerves after this afternoon."

"You got it," Chet said.

"Have fun, you two," Cassie said.

They waved as the couple got into Chet's Audi and drove off.

"That was quite a day," Cassie said to Anna. "Do you absolutely have to leave tonight? Decompressing sounds like a good idea."

"I was thinking the same thing. Maybe I'll leave first thing in the morning instead. I should be okay if I leave at 8:00. That will put me home in plenty of time for the 11:00 Mass. It won't start to get busy in my ice cream shop until the early afternoon."

"Perfect," Cassie said.

"Let's see if Mac is still at the inn before we eat. I'm sure he'll be happy to know that Darren's killer was arrested before he heads back to New Hampshire."

They stopped at the inn and went upstairs to knock on his door, but there was no answer. "That's too bad. I would have liked to deliver the good news in person," Cassie said.

"I'm sure Rick will inform him," Anna said.

They started to walk back toward the staircase when Cassie noticed that the door to one of the rooms on the other side of the corridor was open. She peeked her head inside and found Nora, a member of the cleaning crew, making the bed.

"You're working late," Cassie said.

"Someone requested an early check-in tomorrow, so I'm getting a head start."

Cassie glanced out the window at the sand dune across the street, where several pieces of driftwood art caught her eye.

Anna followed her over to the window. "What are you looking at?"

"Do you see anything unusual on the sand dune?"

Anna squinted her eyes. "Maybe. It looks like a bunch of driftwood, but it's hard to tell from so far away."

"Wait here." Cassie ran downstairs to the library and grabbed a pair of binoculars. Taking the stairs two at a time, she rushed back and returned to the window to examine the dune.

"There are pieces of driftwood scattered across it, but they're painted with blue letters, and it looks like they're arranged in a specific order." She handed the binoculars to Anna.

"I think they spell the word 'Protect,' but I can't make out the letters clearly from this distance.

"Remember the driftwood we found at Darren's studio?" Cassie asked.

"Yes. The pieces had smudged sayings on them. I wonder if he had been working on a driftwood art project for the dune."

"That would make sense, given the theme of the sayings. I remember the three we saw said, 'From above, all is clear,' 'Nature speaks to those who listen.' And 'Sand shifts, but truth remains.'"

We thought they were religious because they talked about seeing things from above, but maybe they were meant to be taken literally," Anna said.

"I'll tell Rick so he can investigate. Right now, I just want to have dinner."

The women picked up Artie in the gift shop, then went

back to Cassie's and put some burgers on the grill. Anna cooked while Cassie took Artie for a walk. Then they settled in and enjoyed dinner.

While they were eating, there was a knock on the door. Cassie opened it to find Jake, who joined the women in the living room. "We have an extra burger," Cassie said. "You're welcome to it."

"Are you sure?" Jake asked.

"Absolutely," Anna said, leaning back in the recliner. "We're stuffed."

Cassie poured Jake some iced tea, and they chatted while he ate.

"I was glad to see your car still in the driveway since I didn't have a chance to say goodbye," Jake said to Anna. "Did you decide to stay in town a little longer?"

"Just until the morning," she said. "We had a busy day."

"Oh, yeah?" Jake asked. "Anything interesting?"

The women chuckled and recounted their adventure.

"Wow! You weren't kidding when you said you had a busy day."

"I'm glad we were able to solve the case before Anna went home," Cassie said.

"So am I. I would have been calling every day for updates, and there's a lot waiting for me when I get back to Seagull Cove." She glanced at the floor, momentarily lost in thought.

Cassie had the sense something significant was going on with her friend. She was about to ask what she meant, but something about the expression on Anna's face caused her not to ask.

"I almost forgot," Jake said. "I heard back from Trudy. She and Kerri are going to come to the inn tomorrow at 1:00.

Kerri thinks she can describe Red well enough for you to draw a sketch."

"That's fantastic news. I'll bring my sketchpad and pencils, and I'll meet you in the library."

"Perfect. Do you want a ride to church tomorrow?" Jake asked.

"Sure. I'll meet you at the inn."

"I'm going to head home. I've had a long day," Jake said.

Cassie and Anna didn't stay up much longer after he left.

The following morning, Cassie and Anna had breakfast at the inn at 7:30 so Anna could be on the road by 8. By then, news of Maya's arrest—and their involvement in it—had spread, bringing a flood of questions to their peaceful breakfast. Even Joel and Elizabeth wanted to hear the story of what happened at Lena's.

As they finished eating, Rick walked in.

"I figured I'd find you ladies here," he said. "I wanted to let you know that Maya gave us a full confession."

"That's great news," Anna said. "I was just about to head back to Seagull Cove."

"That's not all," Rick said. "We investigated the sand dune last night after you called, and it turns out what you saw there was the start of a special project Darren had been working on. Even though he went about it the wrong way, he regretted his disrespect for the dunes, and he was trying to give something back to the community. We found some other items at his studio that outlined the full plan for the project."

"That's bittersweet," Cassie said. "On one hand, it's reassuring to know he was no longer trampling the dunes for personal gain. But on the other hand, it makes his murder feel even more tragically unnecessary."

"On a positive note, if the town approves the project, Lena has agreed to finish it."

"I'm happy to hear that," Cassie said.

"We also spoke with Darren's brother, Scott. He has agreed to reimburse Mac Dalton for the money Darren owed him from Darren's estate."

Rick waved at someone on the other side of the tavern and excused himself to say hello.

The women carried their dishes to the kitchen, and just as Cassie was about to walk Anna to her car, Lena walked in holding a white box with a pink bow.

"Lena," Cassie said, "it's so good to see you. How are you doing?"

"Much better than last night."

"We heard you've offered to finish Darren's project," Cassie said. "I'm glad you're going to do that. It seems fitting."

"It's the least I can do. I'm so glad I caught you both." She handed the box to Anna. "This is for you."

"Thanks, Lena. What is it?" Anna asked.

"I couldn't sleep last night, so I made you something."

Anna took the box to one of the armchairs with the lighthouse-patterned fabric in the foyer and opened it. It contained a driftwood seahorse.

"I remembered the first time we talked that you told me that you were going to buy a similar one from Darren. It's probably not as good as his, but I made it for you."

Anna hugged the young artist. "It's beautiful. This was so thoughtful of you. I can't wait to put it front and center on my mantle."

Lena beamed with pride.

"It's the perfect souvenir for your week in Sand Dune Shores," Cassie said.

"I know you need to get on the road, so I won't take any more of your time," Lena said. "Thanks again for everything."

Cassie walked Anna across the street so she could get her suitcase. Artie was resting in his favorite spot in the sunshine by the slider. Anna bent down to say goodbye to the pup, then she stood and took in the view one last time. "You're building a good life here, Cassie. I'm glad I was able to see it for myself. You're going to solve that case for John, and once you do, you'll be able to fully move forward with your career. I just know it."

The women embraced, and Cassie carried Anna's suitcase to her car. Then she watched Anna drive down Starboard Lane.

After Anna left, Cassie spent some time in the gift shop with Monica and Leslie until Jake picked his parents and her up for church.

When they returned, she took Artie for a long walk before settling in the library with him on her lap, flipping through a magazine while waiting for Jake, Trudy, and Kerri to arrive.

Jake arrived a few minutes early and took the seat across from Cassie. He seemed distracted, and she had a feeling it had to do with what happened at the warehouse. She, too, had been thinking about their almost-kiss.

He hesitated before speaking. "I'm glad we've had the chance to spend time together this week. I always enjoy being with you."

"I do too, Jake. You mean a lot to me."

Her words seemed to give him the courage to continue. "We make a great team. But as much as I enjoy our investigating, now that you're back from your trip and your houseguest is gone, I was hoping we could spend more time together... you know, outside of solving mysteries."

Cassie had thought about this a lot. Jake had proven to be a true friend. Her mother always said that if you want to know how a man will treat you, watch how he treats his mother. And there was no doubt that Jake was a loving son. He was also kind to others, including her father, her brother, and Anna. That meant a lot to her.

"I'd like that too, Jake," she said.

He smiled. "I'd like to take you on a date. Would you like to have dinner next Saturday night?"

"I'd love to."

His grin widened. "Great," he said, just as Trudy and Kerri arrived. "We can make the arrangements as the weekend gets closer," he added quickly, rising to greet them.

Cassie nodded, her heart lighter than it had been in a long time.

After Jake introduced everyone and Artie gave their guests a friendly greeting, they sat at the conference table in front of the window.

"Thank you for agreeing to meet with us," Cassie said.

"We're the ones who should be thanking you," Trudy said. "If you can catch this guy, maybe we can get back the artwork he stole. At the very least, he won't be able to do any more damage."

"In that case, let's get started," Cassie said, picking up a grey pencil and opening her sketchbook.

Kerri described every detail she could remember about the man they believed to be Red. When she finished, Cassie revealed her sketch.

"I'm impressed," Kerri said. "That's exactly how I remember him."

"He certainly has a distinct look," Cassie said, studying her sketch. The drawing depicted a man with straight red hair falling halfway to his shoulders, small but bright blue eyes, and a close-cut beard. He wore a long brown coat and appeared to be in his early forties.

"I'll say," Trudy said.

"That's why I was confident that I'd be able to describe him to you," Kerri said.

"Is there anything else you need from us?" Trudy asked. "I left a couple of my newer employees alone in the gallery, so I need to get back. It's been a busy day."

"That's all," Cassie said. "This was a huge help. Thank you for your time."

They walked them to the door, then Cassie and Jake returned to the library.

Jake picked up the sketchpad and studied the drawing. "This is going to be invaluable as we search for Red," Jake said.

"One thing is for sure—we'll recognize him if we see him."

Jake snapped a picture of the sketch. "I'll show it to Rick, too."

"I'm feeling confident," Cassie said. "Now that we know who we're looking for, it's only a matter of time before we find him."

The End... of Book 4

What's Next?

Cassie's Cape Cod adventures aren't over yet!
A Whale of a Murder (Book 5) is coming in Nov. 2025!

* * *

Make sure you're on Angela's mailing list so you can learn about new releases, sales, and exclusive content. As a thank you gift for joining Angela's Readers' Group, you will receive a free copy of *Vacations and Victims,* the prequel to the *Sapphire Beach Series.*

Available in ebook and PDF formats at:
BookHip.com/BSTWMVC

* * *

While you wait for *A Whale of a Murder,* follow Anna's journey in the *Seaside Ice Cream Shop Mysteries*!

Anna is solving a mystery of her own that even Cassie doesn't know about!

After the tragic death of her sister, Bella, Anna needs a radical change. So, she closes her counseling practice in Boston and moves to a quaint seaside town to open an ice cream shop. But her grand opening ends on a sour note after her musical entertainment turns up dead. In addition, a customer thinks he spotted Bella. What he doesn't know is that Bella's body was never found. Could Anna's sister still be alive?

Paperback bundles and individual books are available at Angela's store.

Visit: **store.angelakryan.com** to save with a bundle.

Individual books are also available on Amazon

ALSO

Meet Connie!

Connie Petretta can think of no other option but to sell the beach front condo she inherited from her beloved aunt, but a murder next door stalls her plans.

If you enjoy page-turner mysteries, endearing characters, and sun-drenched Florida beaches, you'll love the ***Sapphire Beach Cozy Mystery Series!***

Paperback bundles and individual books are available at Angela's store.

Visit: **store.angelakryan.com** to save with a bundle.

Individual books are also available on Amazon.

ABOUT THE AUTHOR

Angela K. Ryan is the author of the *Cape Cod Cozy Mysteries,* the *Seaside Ice Cream Shop Mysteries,* and the *Sapphire Beach Cozy Mystery Series.* She writes clean, feel-good cozies for readers who love humor, lots of twists and turns, and happy-dance endings.

When she is not writing, Angela enjoys the outdoors, especially kayaking, stand-up paddleboarding, snowshoeing, and skiing. She lives in Massachusetts and loves all four of the New England seasons, but looks forward to regular escapes to the white, sandy beaches of southwest Florida, where her mother resides.

Angela would happily live in any of the fictitious seaside towns in Massachusetts and Florida, where her series take place, if it weren't for all the bodies that keep turning up!

Angela dreams of one day owning a Cavalier King Charles Spaniel like the sweet pup in her *Sapphire Beach Series,* but she isn't home enough to take care of one. So, for now, she lives vicariously through one of her main characters, Connie.

Printed in Great Britain
by Amazon

62674723R00099